THE GUNSMITH

#405 BLOOD COAST

THE GUNSMITH #405: BLOOD COAST
A Pro Se Press Publication

Blood Coast is a work of historical fiction. Many of the important historical events, figures, and locations are as accurately portrayed as possible. In keeping with a work of fiction, various events and occurrences were invented by the author.

Edited by Tommy Hancock
Editor in Chief, Pro Se Productions—Tommy Hancock
Submissions Editor—Rachel Lampi
Director of Corporate Operations—Kristi King-Morgan
Publisher & Pro Se Productions, LLC-Chief Executive Officer—Fuller Bumpers

Cover Art by Jeffrey Hayes
Print Production and Book Design by Percival Constantine
New Pulp Logo Design by Sean E. Ali
New Pulp Seal Design by Cari Reese

Pro Se Productions, LLC
133 1/2 Broad Street
Batesville, AR, 72501
870-834-4022

editorinchief@prose-press.com
www.prose-press.com

Published in digital form by Piccadilly Publishing, September 2015

THE GUNSMITH

#405 BLOOD COAST

J.R. ROBERTS

PROSE PRESS

ONE

The fragrant, salty air and warm breeze had nothing at all to do with Jack Mancuso's good mood. Not even a northern California sunset reflecting off the choppy waters of the Pacific played a part in the smile that crossed Jack's face. He simply wasn't the sort of man to take pleasure in such things. What Jack Mancuso liked was money and there was plenty of it to be found on the train steaming north along the coast.

Smiling beneath a dark, bushy mustache, he gazed through a pair of field glasses to watch the train work its way along the tracks. There were only three cars trailing behind the engine, one of which was loaded with coal. The other two looked like passenger cars that could be found on most any train making its way across the country at any given time. But there were no faces gazing out from the windows to take in the scenery. There were no heads resting against the inside of the glass panes, whiling away long hours with much-needed sleep. In fact, none of the shades were drawn on any of the windows on either of the two rear cars and not a single sign of life could be found.

"What do you think, Jack? Is it time to board that train yet or not?"

Mancuso lowered the field glasses and turned to look at the two men who waited nearby. The one who'd asked the question was Nelson Stamp, a lean man with dark black skin and sharp eyes. Nelson didn't ask a lot of questions. He tended not to speak much at all unless it was absolutely necessary, which was an admirable trait in their line of work.

The other man in the group was Terrance Jordan. He looked just as rough and disheveled as a clump of tumbleweed that had blown in from the desert. His short brown hair was the color of dry topsoil and had plenty of the gritty stuff in there as well. His round face was covered in stubble and, despite all the time he spent in the elements, still somehow had a slightly doughy texture. Although he hadn't been the one to ask the question to the group's leader, he shifted in his saddle, anxiously awaiting the reply.

All three men were on horseback, poised atop a ridge that looked down on the green California slopes. The ocean was a few miles away and out of sight, but the wind carried its scent like a message from other lands. Mancuso pulled in a lungful of that message, held on to it for a second, and then let it seep out through clenched teeth.

"Yeah," he said in a low, harsh voice. "It's time."

TWO

Charlie Addard had been driving trains almost as long as there had been tracks connecting one end of the country to the other. He could diagnose a problem within an engine just by listening to it rattle and the scorches on his hands were so deep they were damn near permanent. His eyes narrowed when he stared further down the track in front of him and his lips parted in a silent curse.

"Somethin' wrong, Chuck?" Mark Carroll asked as he pulled open the narrow door leading from the back of the engine.

Charlie didn't respond. Instead, he took hold of the throttle and eased it back.

Mark headed toward the front of the engine. "Why are you slowing down?" When Charlie applied the brakes with enough force to make the wheels squeal, Mark snapped, "What the hell? We got a schedule to keep!"

"We're stopping," Charlie said.

By now, Mark had caught sight of the single horse standing in the middle of the track ahead. "Why don't you just warn him first? Here," Mark said while reaching for the chain connected to the whistle, "I'll do it."

"Step back."

"I'm not about to catch hell when this ride is over just because you're too timid to give a shout at some asshole who don't know where to put his horse."

"Get out of this engine," Charlie warned. "Now."

"Come on, Chuck. When did you get to be so nervous?" The teasing smirk faded from Mark's face when he saw the sawed-off shotgun filling Charlie's hands. The weapon was kept there to guard against robbers and vagabonds. More often than not, Mark forgot the damn thing was even there. At this moment, however, it was impossible to ignore.

"What do you think you're doing?" Mark asked timidly.

"I'm stopping this train and if you've got a brain in that thick goddamn head of yours, you'll jump off before the wheels stop turning."

"Or what?" Mark asked. "You'll shoot me?"

"I'm not gonna shoot you," Charlie sighed. "But I'm not the one you have to worry about."

Mark looked out the window at the man who sat tall in his saddle as the train drew closer to him. That rider looked right back at him as if he was staring down a loudmouthed drunk in a saloon instead of someone behind the controls of a locomotive that could turn him and his horse into paste. Although Mark couldn't see the expression on that man's face, he could just make out the rifle in his hands.

"You can't stop," Mark said. "That was our only order. We're not to stop for anything until we reach our station."

"I know what the order is."

"Then why the hell are you stopping?"

"Because they got my Sophie."

"Who does?" When he didn't get a reply, Mark took the other man by the shoulders and shouted, "Who does, Charlie? Who's got your Sophie?"

Charlie didn't say another word as the train came rattling to a halt. He didn't have to. Mark knew whoever had ridden onto the tracks to stop that train was the one who'd somehow gotten a hold of Charlie's little girl. Even though he didn't share any blood with her, Mark gnashed his teeth at the very thought of anything happening to her.

Reaching for the throttle, Mark said, "Let me do it, then. I'll run him down and we can start looking for Sophie."

"I already know where she is," Charlie said.

"Then we can get her! Hell, we know enough good men on this here train to lead a march to wherever she's bein' held and take her back. Then we can take those filthy bastards to the law. Or better yet, we can string 'em up from the first tree we find!"

Charlie slowly shook his head. "This is how it's got to be. If I don't stop this train and let these men have what they want, they'll send word to have Sophie..." He winced as any man would when he pondered the ways a monster might savage a beautiful girl. "They'll hurt her. And if they aren't heard from before too long, I reckon they'll hurt her then as well. The only way to keep her safe is to stop this train and let them on."

Mark didn't need to ask what those men could want. The train had been chartered by a logging company to bring enough money from their banks in California to pay the workers of half a dozen lumber camps further north. The job had its risks, which was why it had paid so well for a relatively short run. But they weren't completely reliant on the movement of the train to keep its contents secure.

"The guards!" Mark said as if he'd just remembered all the armed men riding as passengers on that train. "They'll..."

Before Mark could take any comfort from the knowledge he'd just regained, the sound of gunshots ripped through the air. The first few came with a second or two between them. After that came some return fire, but not a lot of it. Every little explosion hit Mark's eardrums like a hammer, causing his entire body to twitch.

Charlie barely moved. His head hung low and his body was limp as if he'd already been hit by a fatal round.

Mark waited for the noise to quiet down before chancing a peek outside. The first thing he saw was a lean black man standing outside the car containing most of the guards. Nelson Stamp held a pistol in each hand and fired one last shot into whichever guard was still moving within the car. A few more shots could be heard. Mark didn't see the man who'd fired them, but he knew they came from outside the train instead of anyone still inside. A small bit of hope flew through Mark's head as he weighed his chances of taking Charlie's advice and getting away from that train altogether. The next thing to fly through his mind was a chunk of hot lead from Jack Mancuso's gun.

With smoke still curling from his barrel, Jack grabbed Mark by the collar and pulled him out so the dead man could flop outside the train. Climbing onto the step leading to the engine, Mancuso asked, "You got any keys or anything like that I might need to get to that money?"

Charlie shook his head. "The guards have that sort of thing. All I do is drive."

"And you did a real fine job of that."

Closing his eyes, Charlie said, "My Sophie is to be set free."

"Of course. I ain't got no use for a girl that young. You done real good."

"I was told you wouldn't kill none of those men."

Mancuso made a spitting sound as he tried to suck a bit of his lunch from between his teeth. "I did tell you that. It weren't true, though."

"My Sophie, though. She's all right?"

Mancuso didn't make another sound. He simply waited for the engineer to open his eyes and look up at him. Once he got a chance to stare directly at him, Mancuso pulled his trigger and sent Charlie to hell.

"I'll give that tasty little girl your regards," Mancuso sneered.

THREE

Clint Adams was on his third hour at a poker table in a saloon that could barely stand. The place was at the center of a trading post like the rusty hub of a crooked wheel. He'd started out winning, but when his losses began to pile up he suspected he might be getting fleeced by at least one cheat among the other players. He soon found a way to steer his luck back in the proper direction and built up a small stack of chips in front of him. Those had been whittled away here and there, but not at a pace that he couldn't handle.

If not for the pleasant company around that table, Clint would have pulled up stakes and left some time ago. Instead, he found himself enjoying the conversation and laughing at the crude jokes that were being tossed back and forth. Considering the company he was forced to keep on so many other occasions, that card game was a much needed breath of mostly fresh air. If the price of admission was a few dollars lost here and there, so be it.

"My, my," sighed Clarence Gein, a round fellow with less than a dozen hairs sprouting from his shiny scalp. "What have we here?"

"If you intend on making me turn around so you can try to swipe some of my chips again," Clint warned, "you might want to remember what happened the last time."

Clarence reached up to touch a red lump on the side of his face that had been put there when Clint sent a right hook his way after the first couple minutes of their game. Oddly enough, the incident had been the first of many laughs shared by the entire table. For those who knew Clarence Gein very well, the incident actually wasn't very odd at all.

Paying as much attention to the lump on his face as he did to the gravy smeared beside it, Gein said, "I ain't yanking your chain, Adams. You'll be sorry if you don't take a gander for yourself."

"Nice try, but I'm no fool," Clint said with confidence. He looked around to the others at the table, who were also looking at something behind him. Clint placed a hand on top of his chips, twisted around in his chair, and immediately spotted the source of the other men's attention.

More than likely, the blonde woman was very accustomed to drawing that kind of attention. She wore a light blue dress that was laced tightly up the front to display a trim waist while accentuating pert, rounded breasts. Her golden hair was gathered to fall over one shoulder and was held together with a ribbon that matched her skirts. She smiled at the table of gamblers with softly curved lips that parted a second before she spoke.

"I'm looking for a man," she said.

Gein was so quick to jump to his feet that he nearly upended the table. "I'm a man," he said. "A fact that I can prove to you at your earliest convenience."

She approached the table, placed her hands upon her hips, and said, "Actually, I'm looking for a specific man. His name is Clint Adams."

"Damn it all to hell," Gein snorted as he went through the clumsy process of settling back into his seat.

"You should be a better sport, Clarence," Clint chided. "After all the times I bested you at this very table I would've thought you'd had plenty of practice at losing to me."

Once he'd gotten situated in his chair, Gein picked up a coin from the pile in front of him and sent it whistling through the air with a snap of his wrist. "Take that, Adams," he said as the coin bounced off Clint's chest. "That's about what your opinion is worth to me or anyone else."

"Speak for yourself," one of the other gamblers said. "If Clint's got pretty little things like that comin' round asking for him, I want to hear whatever advice he's got to offer."

"Yeah, yeah," Gein muttered. "She probably just wants to sell him something."

"Whatever she's selling," Clint said as he stepped away from the table, "I'm buying." He looked to the young lady and added, "Within reason, of course."

The woman was already walking away from the table. She turned to glance over her shoulder, wearing an expression that let Clint know she was fully aware of his eyes on her swaying little backside. "I hope I wasn't pulling you away from anything important."

"Did you get a look at the men I was playing cards with?"

"Yes," she replied while taking another look just to be sure.

"Then you should guess there's not a lot of important things going on over there. Even so," Clint added, "I shouldn't stay away too long. I do have money waiting at that table of thieves."

Having reached the bar, the woman turned to face Clint and extend her hand. "My name is Selma Coates."

"Coates?"

"Right," she said. "As in something warm that wraps around you."

"Ahh, yes. On second thought, my money should be safe without me for a while."

FOUR

"So," Clint said as he leaned against the bar. "You found me. Now what?"

"I had some things in mind I wanted to say," Selma told him. "But now that you're right here in front of me, it's difficult for me to keep my thoughts straight."

Her hands had drifted toward Clint's chest and her fingers drifted between the buttons of his shirt. Each nail brushed against him, making it seem as though she could somehow touch him through the coarse cotton.

Clint took hold of her by the wrists and eased her hands back an inch or two. "I'm flattered by the attention," he said, "but there's no need to butter me up. Just say what it is you want to say."

"When I came in here, I had something to ask you. Now," she added in a low, sultry voice, "there's something else altogether that I want to say."

"Yeah?"

Selma grinned, averted her eyes and put on a bashful expression that was cute, if not entirely convincing. "What I want to say is that I need to feel you inside of me."

Clint's eyebrows went up. "Is it, now?"

She nodded. "I want to feel my skin against yours, your hands on me, your cock inside me. God, I'm already wet between my legs just thinking about it."

13

The next minute or two passed in a rush. Clint had already rented a room in the place across the street and he took Selma there as quickly as his legs could carry him. She had no trouble matching his pace and even got ahead of Clint once or twice before they reached his door. At that moment, Clint turned his key in the lock and pushed the door open while Selma shoved him inside.

Since Clint's hands were busy exploring the curves of Selma's body, he shut the door to his room with a solid kick. He didn't bother checking to make sure it remained shut before lifting her off her feet and pinning her against the closest wall. She responded by wrapping her legs around him and holding on so tight that her arms were free to pull Clint's shirt open in one try.

Clint reached down to cup her firm little ass in both hands while pressing her against the wall. Her lips were wet and sweet. Before long, she slipped her tongue into his mouth while moaning softly from the back of her throat. Selma was back on her feet and reaching down to loosen Clint's jeans. As she slid them down over his waist, she pushed him back and dropped to her knees in front of him.

Looking down, Clint saw her soft lips wrap around his cock before she swallowed him whole. When she sucked him, she savored every inch. And when she eased her mouth back again, she let her tongue drift along the sensitive flesh of the underside, to tease him until she bobbed her head forward again. Selma kept that up for a minute or two, which was almost more than Clint could handle.

When he took a step back to catch his breath, Selma remained on her knees. She pulled her skirts up to show the smooth skin of her bare thighs. A little more, and she revealed the thin layer of silk that was her last undergar-

14

ment. Selma turned her back to Clint, got on all fours, and lowered her chest to the ground while lifting her rump a bit higher. "Don't make me wait for it, Clint," she said.

There was no way in hell Clint was going to make her wait for anything. Without the slightest bit of hesitation, he knelt behind her, eased Selma's skirts up a little higher, and guided his rigid pole between her legs. Her pussy was slick and ready for him, accepting every inch of his erection until he was buried all the way inside of her. Clint took her hips in his hands and held on as he started to pump into her with a steady rhythm.

Selma clawed at the floor like a cat, tossing her head back and moaning every time he drove into her. Her first climax approached quickly and seemed to take even her by surprise. She pressed back against him to push him even deeper between her thighs until her entire body trembled with pleasure. Once that passed, Selma was anxious for the next wave.

Clint could feel her pussy clench around him when she was at the height of her orgasm. As soon as she relaxed, he placed one hand on the small of her back and the other on the side of her hip so he could feel her muscles tense when he began pumping into her again. Soon, he reached forward with both hands to cup her firm breasts while pounding into her with even more vigor.

"Yes," she cried. "Give it to me."

He gave her everything he had. Holding on to her with both hands, Clint could feel Selma's nipples grow hard as diamonds against his palms. Her pussy was so slick that he glided in and out of her with ease until finally he reached his own boiling point. Clint exploded inside of her after one last thrust and then dragged himself to the nearby bed.

"Wasn't there something you wanted to ask me?" he said, taking a deep breath.

Selma crawled onto the bed and lay beside him. "Give me a chance to catch my breath," she gasped.

FIVE

There was a narrow door at the back of Clint's room. Instead of a closet, it opened to a small balcony looking down onto a side street. There wasn't much of a view to enjoy, but the space was just big enough for two people to stand in the fresh air with some degree of privacy. Clint leaned against the railing while Selma struck a match against the wall to light the slender cigarette clenched between her teeth.

"Selma Coates," Clint mused.

"Does the name strike you as familiar?" she asked.

"Should it?"

"It might, if you've heard of my father." Selma paused in case Clint would volunteer the name. Since he didn't have much to say on the subject, she blew out some smoke and told him, "Derrick Coates."

That name did strike Clint as vaguely familiar, but only a bit more so than Selma's. There was something that rang a bell in his mind, even if the sound of that bell was a mighty long way off. Suddenly, it hit him. Clint snapped his fingers and said, "Derrick Coates! Of Coates Overseas Shipping."

"That's right," Selma said with a nod.

"That company runs out of San Francisco, doesn't it?" he asked.

"It sure does."

"I would've thought you'd be there," Clint said.

"Why? Because a good daughter should stay close to home in case her daddy needs anything done?"

"Not exactly. I just thought someone like you might find San Francisco more appealing than a little trading post stuck in the middle of a bunch of trees."

The hint of anger that had appeared on Selma's face was gone almost immediately. She smiled and took another pull from her cigarette. "I guess I might have a tender spot when it comes to my father."

Clint was about to mention something regarding a few tender spots he'd found, but decided that wasn't the best time for jokes. Instead, he asked, "Were you looking for me in regards to a matter involving your father?"

"Him and his company, yes. Although, the two might as well be the same damn thing."

"Anyone who builds something that has any worth tends to keep it mighty close," Clint said. "It's a necessary evil, I'm afraid."

Looking Clint over as if she was studying him, Selma asked, "Do you know something about that?"

"I do. I may not have built a company from the ground up, but I've taken part in plenty of important ventures with some important men. It often seems as if the bigger the achievement, the further those men have to distance themselves from friends and family."

"You do know something on the matter," she said with a mildly disgusted sigh. "I wouldn't presume to ask you or anyone else how to handle my father in a familial sense. My proposition has to do with the company."

"I'm listening."

She hesitated a moment, rubbing her upper arms as if suddenly cold.

"I'm afraid something might happen."

"To your father's company?" Clint asked. "But it didn't seem as though you were interested in being a part of that with him."

"Mostly," she said in a measured tone, "I'm afraid that something might happen to me and then, after I'm gone, my father's company."

Clint stood up straight. "All right," he said. "Now I'm really listening."

SIX

It had been a few days since he'd stopped that train, but Jack Mancuso still had the smell of burnt gunpowder in his hair and on his skin. Although he'd wanted to leave it there for a bit longer, the whore he'd bedded talked him into taking a bath and now the smell was gone. The whore was gone too, but there would be another before much longer. Just like there would be more burnt gunpowder.

Mancuso didn't know the name of the town he was in. It was just another shit hole with a saloon and a stable. He passed the latter while on his way to the former, having made the short walk from the cathouse where he'd had his bath. Nelson's room was on the second floor. On his way up, Mancuso bought a bottle of whiskey and drained a good portion of it before knocking on his partner's door.

In the next room, there was a familiar man's voice followed by a woman's giggling. Mancuso couldn't make out exactly what was being said in there and didn't much care. He waited a few seconds before knocking again.

"Damn, Jack!" Nelson said as he opened the door. "You almost busted the door down."

"Then you should have answered it sooner." Mancuso shoved past Nelson as he barged into the room. A busty woman with long brown hair was on the bed with most of a smile still etched onto her face. Her dark brown nipples were still swollen from the attention they'd been getting. Mancuso pointed to her with the bottle in his hand and said, "Get dressed and get the fuck out of here."

"This isn't your room," she scolded. "You can't just..."

Mancuso swatted her across the face with his empty hand. "Talk any more sass to me and you'll get it with the bottle next time. Now get the fuck out."

No stranger to being threatened or even slapped, the woman wasn't about to wait for Nelson or anyone else to defend her honor. It was simpler to just leave while she could, so that was exactly what she did.

"Sorry, sweet thang," Nelson said to her as she passed him on her way to the door. "I'll catch up to you later."

"Don't bother," she spat. "I can find plenty of men who'd be happy to slap you around. See how you like it!"

Mancuso took a step back to let the woman go. He lifted an arm as if he was going to take another swing, but raised it over his head instead. His other arm went up, making him look as if he was being robbed. "You always did know how to pick 'em, Nelson. Maybe I'll take a run at her as well."

The woman moved even quicker to the door. Once she got there, she glanced over her shoulder at Mancuso. No amount of posturing could hide the fear in her eyes when she looked at him. That fear fed something inside Mancuso that brought a wicked grin to his lips.

"Yeah," he said. "I'll definitely hunt you down some-time real soon."

"Stop scaring the ladies," Nelson said while moving toward a pile of his things in one corner of the room. "I know that's not why you barged in here like you owned the damn place."

"You're right about that," Mancuso replied. "How much did you get from that little girl's daddy?"

"You first."

When Mancuso reached into his pocket, he glared at the other man as if he was about to pull death itself from its hiding place. Instead, he took out a wad of money, hefted the weight of the rolled currency and tossed it to Nelson. "That's your cut from the train job," he said. "Plus a little more."

Nelson frowned and then flipped through the money he'd been given. Only then did he ask, "What's the extra for?"

"You done a good job."

"Come on. There's more to it than that."

"Why would you ask such a thing?" Mancuso said with the tone of a man who'd just been slapped in the face.

Without responding to the offense Mancuso had supposedly taken, Nelson replied, "Because I've known you for more than a day and a half. Ain't nothing in this world is free. I believe you told that to someone right before you shot him in the back."

Mancuso pondered that for a few seconds. "Oh yeah," he eventually said. "I guess I did. In Sacramento, wasn't it?"

"I believe so."

"That extra is because there might not be a job for a short spell..."

Now it was Nelson's expression that became darker. "What do you mean? The next job was supposed to already be lined up."

"It was."

"Then what's the delay?"

"Might not even be a delay," Mancuso told him.

Nelson weighed the money in his hand one more time. Despite the satisfying weight of the rolled-up bills, he didn't seem happy when he closed his fist around them and tucked them away into a pocket. "What else is there that I should know?"

"You always were the smarter one," Mancuso said.

"Smart is one thing. Not taking this money without some questions just proves I ain't a damn fool."

"Terrance took his and was quite happy about it."

Nelson raised an eyebrow, knowing he didn't have to say out loud how little both men thought of the third man in their group.

"Yeah, you're right," Mancuso said in response to the words that hadn't needed to be said. "Terrance would be happy with a sack of rocks if they was shiny enough. I may only need one of you on this next job."

"So I guess that one will be me and we can find a bag of rocks to keep Terrance happy."

"Could be I don't even need one more."

"So what the hell are we supposed to do?" Nelson asked. "We all got prices on our heads and the best way to keep anyone from cashing in on us is to keep moving."

"You'll need to stay where I can reach you," Mancuso said. "It may just turn out that this job requires more men after all and if that's the case, I'll need the two of you to get to me in a rush. I can't sit around waiting to see whether or not you got the message I send."

"Or you could tell me where you're headed and I can check in on you to see if you need help. That way I might be able to line up some work on my own."

"Which brings us right back around to you getting that extra money in this payout so you don't have to fret about finding another job of your own."

"Sometimes I think you enjoy talking in circles," Nelson sighed.

"I wouldn't have to if you'd just take what you're given and not ask so many goddamn questions."

"Asking questions is what keeps me alive. Especially when I'm working with the likes of you."

"The likes of me, huh?" Mancuso sneered. "All right, then. I may already have a prime hostage on this next job. So prime that taking this money might just be a matter of walking in, grabbing it, and walking out."

"And if it ain't so easy?"

"Then I might need help."

"Might?" Nelson asked.

"You can be a real trial, you know that?"

"Yeah, I do know. If you just want a man who acts like a lapdog and barks when you tell him to, why not go back to Terrance's room? I imagine he's always ready for a good scratch behind the ears."

"Fine, damn it," Mancuso said. "You made your point. What do you want?"

"I want to come along with you on this job."

"And if I don't need your help?"

Nelson shrugged. "Then you don't have to pay me a cut. I'll take what I've already been so generously given and be done with it."

"What do you get out of a deal like this?"

"I get to be first on the list for reinforcements. Also," Nelson added, "I get to make certain just how juicy this job really is. That way, I can know for certain the cut I'm paid is what it should be and not some figure that was whittled down because nobody bothered to check it."

"You don't even know what this job is."

"All I do know is that it must be real damn good for you to work so hard to keep me and Terrance in the dark about it."

"Damn, I hate you sometimes."

"Do we have a deal?"

"Yeah," Mancuso grunted. "We got a deal."

SEVEN

uilt on ground that was too soggy to be used for farming, the trading post where Clint had spent his last few days always smelled vaguely of mold. In an odd sort of way, that scent mixed with the salty air blowing in from the sea wasn't altogether bad. When there was no wind blowing, however, the smell quickly became overpowering. At those times, most folks sought refuge within the post's saloon or restaurant. The locals who'd lived in that area for most of their lives barely even noticed.

Like most places of its kind, the trading post's saloon served food to its customers. Since there was no other saloon within thirty miles to compete with it, this one didn't bother going to any extra effort to do much more than fill a man's belly. Apart from whatever scraps could be found in the kitchen, beef stew was almost always served. It was too watery and the beef was too fatty, which amounted to a whole mess of grease in the bottom of the bowl. To balance that out, it was served poured over a large chunk of bread that Clint found pretty damn tasty. The bread at the bottom of the bowl he'd just been given hadn't even gotten a chance to soften before he picked up his conversation with Selma where it had left off on the balcony of his room.

"Is this more to your liking?" Clint asked as he motioned to the saloon around him.

Selma nodded. "It was too easy to be overheard before. I could also just be imagining things, though. My nerves have been a little frayed when it comes to this whole affair."

"Now that we're somewhere that our voices don't carry quite as much, why don't you tell me what this whole affair involves?"

When Clint had ordered his stew, Selma only got a roll and a cup of hot tea. She swirled the murky water in her chipped cup and took a deep breath before continuing. "There have been some robberies lately. Perhaps you might have heard about them."

Clint chuckled and used his fork to spear a piece of stringy beef and a mushy potato. "It seems someone is always trying to rob someone else at any given time," he said. "Perhaps you could be a little more specific?"

"The robberies have been connected to large companies. Payrolls, merchandise shipments, ore being carted away from large mines, that sort of thing."

"Those things are always targets ripe for the picking as far as most bandits are concerned. That's why there are usually armed guards accompanying them."

"True," Selma said. "But the first ones being targeted in these recent robberies aren't the guards and it's not even the owners of those companies. It's the owners' families."

"Ahh. Now it's getting a little clearer."

Selma nodded. "My father's company is just about to deliver several large shipments. Once they're put onto the boats bound for Europe, payment will be made."

"And you're worried that, whoever these robbers are, they'll come after your father's family? You, in particular."

"It's not just a worry, Mister Adams."

"Please, after all we've recently done to each other, you can call me Clint."

Selma glanced from side to side and flushed slightly in the cheeks.

Shrugging, Clint took another bite of his stew. "I thought you weren't worried about anyone overhearing us."

Meeting his eyes as if to prove she wasn't embarrassed in the least, Selma said, "There could be dangerous men looking for me right now, Clint."

"What makes you so certain of that?"

"Because my father makes it his business to keep an eye open for any threats to his prosperity and he got a report from some Pinkerton men that the robbers in question were in California."

"Lots of rich men in California," Clint offered.

"Not all of them get letters threatening their family."

"You might be surprised."

Selma took a sip of her tea along with a moment to collect herself. "The letter my father received was very specific in intent and very...descriptive as to what would happen to me when they took me."

"When was that supposed to be?" Clint asked.

"Soon. Look, I know men like my father get a lot of threats from all sorts of people. This letter isn't just another empty promise, Clint. I know it. There were things in there, depraved things, that make me want to take it very seriously."

Clint's eyes narrowed so he could block out more of the world around him and study Selma even more carefully. "What about your father? Doesn't he take it seriously?"

Selma didn't have an answer for that. For a few seconds, she didn't even move a muscle. When she did, it was only to lift her cup to terse lips and drink another taste of hot tea.

"He doesn't know about it, does he?" Clint asked.

"Not this more recent letter," she said. "No."

"Why not?"

"Because he might overreact." For a moment, Selma held on to her teacup even though it was already resting safely on the table in front of her. Clint gave her those moments to chew on whatever was running through her mind. When they expired, she looked to him and said, "I left San Francisco so my father wouldn't have to worry about me. The note I left told him that I'd gone to the family cottage in Virginia where I couldn't be found by anyone other than more family."

"Sounds like a sensible plan," Clint said.

"It would be if everyone at the company who might see that letter or hear my father talking could be trusted." Leaning forward, she added, "I've read some newspaper stories that say these robbers might have ears within these companies they steal from. That's how they find out where to get a hold of the people they kidnap."

Clint nodded in agreement as he shoveled some more stew into his mouth. He was just getting to the part of the bread that had soaked up the most gravy and grease. It was beyond words.

"It could be that I'm no safer in Virginia than I am here," she said. "If the wrong men know where I am, I could be in even more danger!"

"I agree."

"Good."

"A thousand dollars."

Selma blinked rapidly as if the shot she'd been dreading had just been fired directly in front of her. "What did you say?"

"You heard me. A thousand dollars."

"For what?"

"For the job you're about to offer me."

Selma sat up straight and placed her hands flat upon the table. "What makes you think I was going to do something like that?"

"Honestly?"

"All right," she said without trying to maintain the charade she'd started. "A blind man could tell where this was leading. A thousand dollars sounds fair. So what do you say?"

"I say San Francisco is a hell of a town and it's been way too long since I've been there."

EIGHT

The trading post may have been stuck in a wide patch of nowhere, but too many people passed through for Clint's liking. If he was going to keep an eye on Selma, the job would be much easier on some more familiar territory. For that reason, along with some personal ones, Clint insisted on heading to San Francisco as soon as he could gather the supplies needed for a ride.

Ironically, the store, which was the main reason the trading post had been built, was the last place Clint had visited during his stay. His arms were full of a sampling from nearly every table and shelf in his sight. Feed, cans of beans and peaches, rope, bacon, matches, and a new bedroll to replace one that had fallen apart in a rain storm filled his arms as he made his way to the front of the store. His eyes fixed firmly on the cash register at the front of the place, Clint cinched his arms around his haul and took careful steps.

Within seconds, he could feel the items he'd chosen start to shift like a pile of rocks just before a landslide. When it became clear there was no stopping the inevitable tumble, Clint hurried to the counter where the owner of the store sat and watched.

"Damn it!" Clint snapped as the bedroll and a few cans of peaches slipped from his grasp to clatter onto the floor. He stooped down to snag the bedroll with one hand, but a few of the cans had already rolled out of his reach.

"Looks like you could use some assistance," a man said as he trapped one of the cans under his boot.

"Much obliged, Mister," Clint said as he tried to get a better grip on his items before they all wound up on the floor. "I seem to have bitten off a bit more than I can chew."

"I've had that problem once or twice myself. Go on and get your load to the cash register. I'm right behind you."

Clint made his way to the front and set his items down on the counter while glaring intently at the spindly young fellow sitting on the other side of it.

"I was just about to come around and help you," the cashier said with a helpless shrug. "Honest."

"Yeah," Clint grunted as he reached down to keep a bundle of jerked venison from slipping off the counter. "I'm sure you were."

If the younger man was truly concerned with maintaining the appearance of someone who truly cared for his customers, he didn't show it. Instead, he started picking through Clint's haul and smacking his fingertips against the keys of his register. Clint was surprised to see the newly patented cash register in a place like this.

Turning to the man behind him, Clint said, "I appreciate the help."

The man who'd leant a hand was about the same height as Clint with a round, friendly face and brown, scruffy hair. He showed Clint half a smirk while nodding toward the pile of goods being added up by the cashier. "Looks like you're getting ready for a long ride."

"Sure am."

"Where you going?"

"North," Clint replied.

"That's it? Just...North?"

"I go where the wind takes me."

After a short nod, the man said, "I reckon you could pretty much make it all the way to San Francisco with that much supplies."

Clint studied the other man a bit more carefully. "Do I know you?"

"Nah. I've just got that kind of face, you know?" the man said, with a smile. "You were hired by that pretty rich lady, right?"

The tapping of the register's keys stopped for a moment. When Clint looked to see what was going on, he saw a hungry look in the shopkeeper's eyes. "Don't get any ideas about marking up the prices, now," Clint warned. "I'm not anywhere close to rich."

"Hadn't crossed my mind," the cashier said unconvincingly. "Honest."

Turning back to face the man behind him, Clint asked, "What's your name, Mister?"

"Don't worry about that," the man replied. "I know you were hired by Selma Coates. Tell me where she is and we can part on friendly terms."

"I may owe you a favor for helping me earlier," Clint said, "but it's not that big of a favor. Accept my thanks and let that be the end of it."

"Wish I could, friend, but I'm afraid I gotta insist." His look turned nasty. "Tell me where to find Selma Coates or things get nasty."

"Doesn't sound like any friends I've ever had," the cashier said in a trembling voice.

Tensed and ready for a fight, Clint said, "Wish I could say the same."

NINE

"**N**ow I know where I recognize you!" Clint said. "You're Terrance Corman, right?"

"Jordan. It's Terrance Jordan."

"I was close. You still riding with those idiots who robbed those mail wagons?" Before he got an answer to his question, Clint glanced over to the nervous cashier and explained, "This man here is an outlaw. Him and his gang got the brilliant idea to hold up a wagon carrying some deeds and other valuables to be delivered to Austin."

"Enough," Terrance warned.

"Only problem was," Clint said without paying the least bit of attention to that warning, "they robbed the wagon when it was on its way back from making its delivery. The deeds and everything had already been dropped off. I suppose none of those geniuses bothered to wonder why the wagon was headed in the wrong direction before they pulled their guns and went to work."

"I said that's enough, Adams! Tell me where to find Selma Coates!"

"Why do you want to know? Are you the one who threatened her?" Intending to pry some bit of information from Terrance by goading him, Clint could tell the other man wasn't quite ready to make a slip of the tongue just yet. To grease those wheels, Clint added, "But I heard those threats were made in a letter and I doubt a man with your brain could read or write."

That was all the grease those particular wheels needed.

Terrance shoved Clint against the counter and reached for his gun. Rather than resist the motion, Clint rolled with it while also rolling over the top of the counter. His boot scraped the cash register on his way over and he forced the young clerk back against the wall before he flopped onto the floor.

Having already committed himself to his own attack, Terrance fired a quick shot through the empty space where Clint had been standing. The shot roared through the confined space of the store and gritty smoke filled the air. Wood splinters rained down onto Clint's shoulder as that bullet dug a hole through the wall.

Twisting around so he wasn't lying on his side, Clint met the clerk's petrified gaze and said, "You might want to keep your head down."

The clerk had moved with impressive speed to get down quickly and didn't even seem capable of standing up again. He barely seemed capable of nodding and grunting his agreement to Clint's request.

Just as he was thinking of the best way to stand up again, Clint was given a golden opportunity by Terrance himself. The gunman leaned over the counter to get a look at where Clint had landed. He led with his gun and as soon as that smoking barrel came into view, Clint reached up for it. His fingers closed around the middle of Terrance's pistol, trapping most of the gunman's hand as well. He tightened his grip as he pulled Terrance over the counter.

Even though the younger man hadn't been taken completely off his feet, he looked more than a little surprised to have come so far. Clint added to his surprise by pounding his fist straight into Terrance's round, gawking face. Before Clint could follow up with a second punch, he was forced to use both hands to keep Terrance from jamming a gun barrel down his throat. It took all of Clint's strength to not only stop the gun from being pointed at him, but shove it in another direction before its hammer was dropped. When it spat its second round, the pistol temporarily washed away every other sound in Clint's ears with a blaring howl.

For the next few minutes, Clint could hear nothing but his own thumping heart and the breaths being pulled in and shoved out of his lungs. The impact of his fist against Terrance's face made a distant thump as he punched the younger man again and again while working his way up and over the counter. The pistol's trigger was pulled again, sending a third round into the wall. The one directly after that shattered some jars on a nearby shelf.

Terrance's face contorted into a strained, vaguely angry expression and his lips peeled back, which was the only way Clint knew he was trying to say something. It was probably just another vicious threat so Clint didn't even bother trying to figure out anything beyond that.

While Terrance was busy putting his next useless string of words together, Clint twisted the younger man's gun hand in the wrong direction. Terrance's pained yelp made it through the thrumming noise filling Clint's ears and his eyes widened as the gun was taken away by force.

For a moment, Clint was too busy juggling the gun he'd taken to draw the gun on his hip. It was only a moment, but that was long enough for Terrance to surprise him. It may have been a stroke of luck that Terrance's timing had been so perfect, but that didn't matter. All that did matter was that Terrance had a holdout pistol strapped to his left ankle and he'd drawn it while stumbling away from the front counter.

Clint lived and died by the gun. He was familiar with a pistol's weight, its grip and most importantly, its balance. If he tried to rush a shot at that moment, the balance would be so awkward that the damn thing might just slip from his hand altogether. Rather than risk a potentially fatal misstep while climbing over the counter or waste a shot on what he knew would be a total miss, he dove past the register toward the closest aisle.

More thumping filled the air as Terrance fired while putting some distance between himself and the counter. Clint felt more than heard those along with the heavy impacts of desperate feet against the floor. Uncertain of exactly how many rounds were left in the pistol he'd taken from Terrance, Clint tossed it aside. By the time he got his legs beneath him and jumped to his feet, Clint had drawn the modified Colt from the holster at his side.

Terrance was at the door, backing away while aiming a little .32 from the hip. In that instant, Clint saw a perfect shot he could take. He also saw through the store's front window that there were people on the street around and behind Terrance; people who might get hit by a bullet that flew through the window or even through Terrance himself.

Clint held his fire, waiting for a second chance that never came. Before he got one, Terrance ducked out of the store and ran away.

The single, angry word that Clint snarled mixed with the ringing in his ears.

TEN

"You let him get away?" Selma asked as the color drained from her face.

Less than an hour had passed since he'd crossed paths with Terrance at the store and Clint had barely stopped moving in that time. After getting back to Selma again and making certain she wasn't in any immediate danger, he'd told her what had happened.

"I didn't let him get away," Clint explained.

"But he got away. Isn't that right?"

"I went after him, but he must've ducked into an alley or into one of those tents set up on the street or behind one of those wagons parked all over this place. How the hell should I know?"

Selma stood with her back against the wall of the stable in the same rigid stance she had since he'd first led her there to prepare for their ride. Her arms were crossed tightly over her chest and her lips were pressed into a firm line. "You could have gone after him."

"I did!"

"And you could have followed him for more than a few seconds."

Choking back the urge to snap at her, Clint said, "He took off at a dead run. There were at least a dozen places he could have gone when he left and I had one chance to guess the right one. I took the best guess I could and

41

didn't see him. After that, he only had that much more time to get away. And before you ask again, yes, I did search for a while longer before coming back here."

Selma let out a terse breath and nodded. "All right. I believe you."

"Great. I suppose I should be honored."

"Don't be like that, Clint. It just...would have been nice if you could have gotten him here and now. Then this whole thing could have been over. I'm sorry."

"I agree on one count," he said. "It would have been nice. I doubt that would have been the end of it, though."

"Why?"

"Because I sincerely doubt he was working alone."

Selma's eyes grew wide and she reached for something to steady herself. Her hand found the edge of the gate to Eclipse's stall. Whether the Darley Arabian stallion sensed the tension in the air or not, he relieved a small bit of it by nuzzling her hand with his nose.

"How many others were there?" Selma asked.

"There was just the one man," Clint replied. "Like I told you. It just seemed pretty clear that he was acting on orders from someone else. Gotta be that man who sent your father the letter, right?"

Nodding, she turned toward the stall so she could rub the side of Eclipse's head.

"Must be," she commented. "How many do you think there are?"

"Hard to say."

"Do you think they're all here?"

Clint approached Eclipse's stall as well, where he was immediately recognized by his faithful companion of so many years. When he looked into the stallion's eyes, Clint couldn't help but recall Eclipse's predecessor. Like any close friend, whether he stood on two legs or

42

four, Duke would always be sorely missed.

"If they were all here," Clint replied, "I imagine more than one of them would have come at me. On the other hand, what happened back at that store seemed more like a warning than a genuine attack."

"Oh good lord," Selma sighed.

"If there are more of them here, whether it was all or just a few others from that gang," he said, "it's a safe bet that they'll come at us again and they won't be trying to hide their numbers."

"Please, Clint," she pleaded. "Let's get back to my father's place in San Francisco. Once I'm there, we'll both be a lot safer."

He thought about it a moment, then said, "It's a few days ride to get there."

"It would be shorter by train."

Normally, Clint preferred to do his traveling by horse instead of by rail. It allowed him to keep as much control as possible on all elements, cut down on the things that might go wrong, from the route taken to any dangers encountered along the way. Once armed pursuers were tossed into the mix, those dangers grew in number. A train did have its own set of advantages as well, however.

Nodding his agreement slowly, Clint said, "That would be faster."

"A lot faster," Selma said, jumping onto to idea excitedly. "Also, I haven't been on a train for some time. Perhaps," she added while approaching him and placing her hands flat upon Clint's chest, "we could get one of those compartments with a bed in it?"

"You just talked me into it."

ELEVEN

"**W**ell, well," Jack Mancuso chuckled when he saw Terrance Jordan step into the small room that was just large enough to host a small card game, "don't you just look like absolute shit?"

Stuck in the back of the saloon, the room was more of a corner sectioned off from the rest by two partitions and a piece of hanging sack cloth for a door. Hearing those words brought a sneer to Terrance's face.

"You get the job done at least?" Mancuso asked.

"Not quite."

Slowly, Mancuso laid down his cards. He drummed his fingers on them and said, "The rest of you, get out."

All four of the other men sitting at his table followed the command like a bunch of tin soldiers that had been wound up and pointed toward the door. Once they'd filed out and left both outlaws alone, Mancuso hooked a finger at Terrance and said, "Come over here."

Terrance moved closer.

"Explain," Mancuso said.

"There was someone else with her," Terrance said, holding his ground firmly.

"Come. Here."

Reluctantly, Terrance moved even closer to the table. The instant he was within Mancuso's reach, he was grabbed by the collar and pulled down with enough force to knock his chin against the top of the cards that had been folded a few seconds ago. By the time Terrance straightened up again, Mancuso was on his feet.

"Tell me the other man looks worse than you," Mancuso snarled.

"'course he does."

"Is he still breathin'?"

"I think so." When he saw the look in Mancuso's eyes, Terrance was quick to add, "Yeah. He is. Unless he fell off his horse or something."

Mancuso's nostrils flared and his eyes narrowed into slits. He reached out for Terrance again, only this time he draped an arm around his shoulders instead of slamming him into any nearby furniture. Cinching in his grip while shaking the other man a bit, Mancuso said, "You always were a funny guy! That's why I keep you around."

"I delivered the message, Jack," Terrance said through an uncomfortable smile. "Near as I could tell, there was only the one man watching over that woman."

"And she was there too?"

"Oh, yeah."

"You saw her?" Mancuso asked.

Terrance nodded as he thought back to the pair of times he'd spotted Selma Coates walking from one section of the trading post to the other. At the time, his eyes had been focused more on the sway of her hips and the bounce in her breasts than where she was actually going, but he knew it was her all right.

"Who was the man that was watching over her?" Mancuso asked. "One of the boys from her daddy's company? Did you at least find that much out?"

"N-no. I don't think so."

"You didn't get a name?"

"I did ask around about him," Terrance replied. For a moment, he considered leaving it at that. But then he considered what Mancuso's reaction might be if he found out that something had been kept from him. Preferring to face consequences now rather than later, Terrance said, "Clint Adams. That was his name."

Mancuso's face darkened as he said, "Nelson's around here somewhere. Find him. Bring him back. We got some plannin' to do."

TWELVE

There was a tent at the trading post with a telegraph and a board displaying the most recent times for departures and arrivals through the closest train station. Since that station was eleven miles away, Clint figured the information was accurate enough. Since San Francisco was the largest city anywhere near the trading post, there were plenty of choices available for him and Selma. Clint settled on one leaving just past noon the following day.

After a quiet night and an uneventful ride the next morning, Clint was loading Eclipse onto a stock car. The Darley Arabian had been on plenty of trains, but seemed a little skittish this time around. He kept shying away from entering the car until Clint put a little force into it.

"I know just how you feel, big boy," Clint said, as he fed Eclipse some oats from his outstretched hand. "I'm not all that happy about being cooped up in this thing, either." He patted the horse's massive neck, trying to comfort him. "But something tells me this is going to be better than us being out in the open."

The young man waiting in the car had Eclipse's stall ready to receive its four-legged guest. "You ready to hand him over?" he asked. "Or would you like to have a few more words with him?"

Clint smiled and gave a tentative laugh. "Not really talking to him. Just...well...I guess I am."

"No need to explain," the liveryman said. "I'll be talking to him as well somewhere during the trip, I reckon. They're damn good listeners."

"Sure are. I appreciate you taking good care of him along the way." With that, Clint flipped a half dollar through the air.

The liveryman caught it and immediately tossed it back. "My pleasure, Mister. It's my job after all. And I ain't had a horse this nice in my charge in a long time."

"It's good to see someone who takes pride in what they do." Tipping his hat, Clint turned on his heel and walked along the side of the train toward the steps extending into the closest passenger car.

The liveryman watched him go and then shifted his attention to Eclipse. Reaching out to pat the Darley Arabian's side, Nelson Stamp whispered, "Yeah, I'll take real good care of you, boy. Might even take you for my own once your friend out there is put into the ground."

THIRTEEN

If there was one surefire way to get killed, Clint knew, it was to ignore a good set of instincts. His instincts were pretty damn good. Surviving for so many years with so many idiots gunning for him for no good reason was proof enough for that. But nobody was perfect and even Clint's instincts had their blind spots. Sometimes, there simply wasn't much of anything to pick up. For those occasions, it served him well to have a backup plan.

Eclipse was more than just fast. He was brave and smarter than most men that crossed Clint's path. The Darley Arabian also wasn't quick to get nervous so when he fretted while being loaded onto that train, Clint knew something was wrong. He couldn't quite put his finger on it just yet, but he trusted the stallion's instincts. After all, it wasn't called horse sense for nothing.

As he stepped back onto the train and into the passenger car, Clint was a coiled spring. His muscles were tensed beneath a relaxed expression and easy stride. His hand twitched imperceptibly whenever it neared the holster at his side, but he continued to swing his arms in time to his steps. His eyes remained pointed straight ahead like any of the others who were concerned with nothing more than finding a seat before the train left the station. All the while, however, he used the edges of his field of vision to watch for anything that might be a hostile move coming toward him.

As would be expected on any train preparing to depart, there was plenty of movement to be found. He spotted plenty of guns hanging at men's sides, but nothing that could be considered out of the ordinary. Clint jumped a bit when he felt a tap on his shoulder, but that was only due to tightly wound nerves and a diligent conductor.

"Ticket, sir?" the man in the blue cap asked.

Clint showed the conductor a flicker of a grin and produced his ticket.

After punching the slip of paper, the conductor said, "Your companion is waiting for you that way, sir."

"What?" Clint asked, his nerves drawing even tighter within his skull.

The conductor, not knowing how close he was to having a very bad day, nodded toward the other end of the car. "The young woman back there," he said. "She told me to let you know where she was."

When Clint looked in that direction, he found Selma standing near the door that led outside to the next car. She waved at him and motioned for Clint to hurry.

"Right," Clint said.

The conductor glanced up from the messy bundle of papers in his hands so he could wink at Clint. "She insisted on getting a private compartment," he said with a wink.

"Yeah. Thanks."

"If you need anything, let me know."

Now Clint was on his way down the narrow aisle running straight through the passenger car. "I should be just fine on my own, thanks."

Without making the slightest attempt to disguise his envy, the conductor said, "Have a good trip, sir," and continued making his collections.

Selma didn't even wait for Clint to get to her before she opened the door and stepped out of the car. The train's engine was beginning to stir and the entire locomotive rattled as it was locked down in preparation for departure. The conductor shouted for Clint's door to be closed as well, but his warning was cut off when Clint stepped outside to join Selma.

"It's right in here," she said while stepping over the connection between cars so she could open the next door. "We'd better hurry before we get into trouble."

"You found us a private compartment?" Clint asked.

"Just one that didn't have anyone else in it yet. If we get there and lock the door, we can keep anyone from disturbing us."

"Sounds good."

The door she'd just opened led to a cramped hallway that ran the entire length of the car to a similar door on the other end. There were six small doors, three on either side, running the length of the car. Selma went to the middle door on the left, opened it, and ducked inside.

"Come on!" she said with an excited giggle.

Clint's nerves jangled anxiously as he passed the first two doors while making his way down the hall. His ears strained to hear someone lurking behind one of those doors preparing to leap out at him. His feet even pressed against the floorboards for an extra amount of time as if he could feel the weight of a gunman drawing near. But all he could hear was the chugging of the engine at the front of the train. All he felt was the lurching of the car as its iron wheels started to turn.

When he got close enough to the middle door, Clint was grabbed by the arm and pulled into a sleeper compartment. There was a square window on the wall marking the midway point between two narrow bunks. Allowing Selma to drag him inside, Clint shut the door behind him and turned the lock.

"That's right," Selma purred as she slowly pulled the string that closed the front of her blouse. "I want you all to myself."

Clint looked past her as he stepped forward. But Selma's eyes had already drifted below his waist and her hand reached for his buckle as he drew near. She didn't notice anything was amiss until Clint took hold of her by the shoulders and moved her aside.

"Hey!" she said. "What are you doing?"

"I need to check on something outside."

"What do you need to check that's better than what's inside?"

Standing at the window, Clint opened it and leaned to get a look at the exterior of the train. "You just need to stay in here and don't open the door for anyone but me," he said.

"But..."

Clint turned around to find her standing with her blouse hanging open and a confused frown on her face. The smooth skin of Selma's chest was exposed by the blouse that had been opened far enough to show the edges of her nipples. "I'd much rather stay in here with you," he said. "Believe me."

"Then stay," Selma purred.

Before he was swayed by a different set of instincts, Clint said, "I'll be right back," before climbing out the window.

"Wait! What are you doing?"

FOURTEEN

The station where Clint and Selma had boarded the train wasn't much more than a few shacks connected to a rickety platform. Once the train pulled away to leave all the structures behind, Clint had plenty of room to do some climbing. It would take a few minutes for everyone inside the train to adjust to all the noise and motion going on around them, providing Clint with more than enough cover to get to the roof of the train without being detected.

He grabbed on to the edge of the roof, placed both feet on the ledge of his window and pulled himself up. The hardest part was finding a handhold up past the ledge. Once his fingers dug beneath some loose shingles, Clint hoisted his lower body up and over. All the while, he could hear Selma trying to catch his attention from within their compartment. She'd started off asking what the hell he thought he was doing and then quickly moved to begging for him to come back.

Stretching over the edge of the roof, Clint looked down to find her leaning out through the window to check on his progress. "I'm all right," he told her.

"What are you doing?" she asked in a harsh whisper that could barely be heard above the growing amount of rushing wind brushing against the train on all sides.

"Making sure there's nobody on this train..." Clint clamped his mouth shut and rolled back onto the roof so he could lay flat and pass below the arm of a coal dump.

As soon as he rolled back to look down at her, Selma said, "Of course we're not the only ones on this train!"

"I'm making sure nobody on this train is gunning for us."

"Oh." Looking back into the compartment behind her and then outside again, she asked, "Wouldn't it be easier to walk inside the train instead of on top?"

"Just get back inside and stay there," Clint said. "Remember what I said about keeping anyone out but me."

"All right."

After Selma disappeared inside once more, Clint expected to see her soon after. She stayed put, however, leaving him to continue his little stroll outside the train.

It wasn't long before the motion of the train smoothed out to something more manageable. The engine was still bringing the locomotive up to speed, but the cars were rattling at a good pace and the bumps in the track were becoming less of a jarring experience for a man trying to cling to the roof like a tick. Having reached the end of the car, Clint drew his legs up under him so he could lift himself into a standing position.

Keeping his hands stretched to either side, Clint stooped down to keep a low center of gravity and inched to the edge of the roof. Once there, he hunkered down even lower before springing from both legs and launching himself over the gap between the two cars. He wasn't airborne for long, but Clint had more than enough time to ponder just how bad his landing could turn out before his boots got anything solid beneath them again. As soon as he reached the next car, Clint allowed his momentum to drop him into a squatting position and stayed there until he regained his balance.

Jumping to the car after that one wasn't nearly as bad and when he landed atop the stock car, he barely broke his stride. Clint's eyes were set on the hatch covering a square vent in the livery car's roof. The opening was there to give the horses some fresh air and to get a bit of the animal smell out of the train. For the moment, however, it was a perfect way for Clint to get another look at the man who'd rubbed against the grain of Eclipse's instincts.

Clint lay on his belly, held his hat in one hand, and peered down through the opening. It looked straight down onto the middle of the livery car, allowing him to see the edges of two stalls. Along with that, he could see two men shuffling back and forth as they paced within the cramped confines of the car. Once again, Eclipse turned out to be a hell of a lot more than one of the finest horses riding the plains.

"That ain't no excuse," a man within the car said.

"What the hell do you want from me?" Although Clint couldn't see the man who spoke those words, he recognized the voice as belonging to the fellow who'd received Eclipse in the livery car. "All I can do is search the train the best I can! I told you Adams and that bitch are here so that means they're here. Finding exactly where the hell they are is just a matter of time."

"Well, you tell that to Jack when he comes along."

The voice of the second man now struck a chord with Clint as well. The last time he'd heard it had been during and after a fistfight in a dry goods store. Terrance Jordan's voice had a distinctly whiny undertone that made it fairly clear that he still felt some of the sting from the beating Clint had handed to him earlier.

A door at the far end of the car was opened and someone stepped inside. From his angle above the other men, Clint could see an entire outline in shadow on the floor before he got a glimpse at the person who'd cast it. Jack Mancuso strode to the edge of Clint's line of sight as if he knew he was being watched from above. His face was hidden by the hat he wore, but he was tall enough to come a bit too close to the car's roof for Clint's liking.

"Tell me what?" Mancuso asked. His hands were propped on his hips as he shifted to look at the other two men in turn. "What the hell do you two look so surprised for? Did you forget we was supposed to meet here?"

"We didn't forget, Jack," Nelson said.

"Then why'd you start without me?" Taking off his hat to reveal a scalp that was so bare it could have been polished to a shine, Mancuso asked, "What'd I miss?"

"Clint Adams is aboard," Nelson reported. "So is Selma Coates."

"I knew that already. Hell, that's why we're all here. What else have you got for me?"

After a stretch of silence that bordered on becoming uncomfortable, Terrance added, "They're bound for San Francisco."

It was all Clint could do to stop himself from announcing his presence by busting into laughter. He managed to keep his mouth shut, but it wasn't easy.

Mancuso, on the other hand, wasn't as amused. "We're all bound for San Francisco, you fucking idiot!" he roared. "Aw fer Christ's sake. Just tell me where to find them and I'll do the goddamn work."

"They're in one of the sleeper cars," Terrance replied.

"Which one?"

"I'm...umm...not sure."

Looking to Nelson, Mancuso asked, "Is that true?"

Nelson lifted his hands reflexively, as if to ward off an imminent attack. "For right now, yes."

"That's the part you weren't happy about telling me when I walked in here?"

"Yeah. Pretty much."

"Smart man. Now I want you to walk straight back through all them passenger cars and see who's in those seats. If them two ain't there, keep going to the sleepers and knock on every door. Look in every room. If someone doesn't open their door, kick it down. Find Selma Coates. Shoot whoever is standing guard over her. That easy enough for ya?"

"Yes, sir," both other men said in unison.

FIFTEEN

Clint had heard a lot of threats in his time. Most were just a bunch of wind that didn't carry any more weight than a belch that had been stretched out over a few seconds and delivered through a sneer. Others weren't made for the purpose of putting on a show. They were simple statements of intent made by someone with the ruthlessness to see them through. Having been on the receiving end of so many threats, Clint could spot the differences between them fairly well. The words he'd heard from Mancuso sent a cold wave through him.

If he didn't move quickly, Clint knew that Selma would be found and she would be hurt. As much as he wanted to drop through the roof of the stock car with guns blazing, he knew that would be a potentially fatal mistake. There wasn't much room to maneuver in that car and the space would most likely fill up with flying lead in under two seconds. That combination wouldn't end well for the one man who'd be the focal point of most of that gunfire.

So Clint ignored his instinct and bided his time. He got to his feet slowly, choosing stealthy movement on top of the train rather than getting a target in his sights as quickly as possible. Terrance and Nelson stepped out of the stock car so they could cross into the one connected to it and Clint hunkered down like a wildcat perched on a branch high above its next meal.

The sound of iron brushing against tooled leather caught Clint's ear, rustling through the current of rushing wind and churning pistons.

"Put that damn thing away," Nelson snapped. "No need to stir anything up until it's necessary."

"Adams is on this train and he's with that Coates woman," Terrance said. "You don't think it's necessary to be ready for him?"

"Ready for him, sure. That don't mean we tip our hand and turn everyone on this train against us before we got what we came for."

"Who do we really got to worry about? You tellin' me you're afraid of a bunch of city folk and old timers? Because that's mostly who I saw in these passenger cars."

Stopping with his hand on the door leading into the next car, Nelson said, "It don't take a gunfighter to pull a trigger and there are plenty of triggers in there."

"True. And all it takes is one or two of them to get a few lucky shots in to make things tough."

Nelson's hand snapped out to swat the side of Terrance's head. "All we need is for some of them folks to get nervous enough to fire a shot and bring the real trouble straight to us. Don't you know who Clint Adams is?"

"I've heard the name."

"Then you shouldn't be anxious to fight him."

"What's the matter?" Terrance asked with bravado that felt as solid as a bridge made from wet newspapers. "You afraid of him?"

"Afraid's got nothing to do with it. Anyone who's chomping at the bit to go against a man like Adams has got shit for brains. You want to draw that kind of fire?"

Nelson asked as he let go of the door and stepped to one side. "Be my guest."

Although Terrance reached for the door, he didn't go so far as to take hold of it. Once he got within an inch of the slightly rusted handle, he let out a prolonged breath and nodded. "You're right. Go on ahead and lead the way. I'll cover you."

Whether he was tired of debating or just sick of looking at the other man's face, Nelson yanked open the door and stepped into the passenger car. The noise in between the two cars was a constant roar of rushing wind, clattering wheels, and the churning engine up ahead. It wasn't quite loud enough to wash out the men's voices, but it had been more than enough to mask the sound of Clint's boots upon the roof of the stock car.

When Clint's foot pressed down on the edge of the roof, a rusty squeak pealed through the air. Terrance looked up at the sound, but was too late to do anything to avoid what was coming for him. All of Clint's body was behind his left boot as he swung down to smash his heel against the side of Terrance's face. After the beating he'd given Terrance before, Clint almost felt bad for adding a new set of bruises to the mix.

Almost, but not quite.

Terrance staggered back, his hands reaching out for the door as well as the gun at his side. The moment Clint landed with both feet on the platform between the two cars, he shut the door to the passenger car and lunged at the man he'd used as a cushion for his landing.

"What the hell?" was all Terrance managed to say before a swift uppercut knocked him into the railing separating him from the passing landscape.

Clint followed up with another uppercut that packed even more wallop than the first. Reeling from the blow and still confused by what was going on, Terrance fell over the railing and off the train completely to land in a patch of tall weeds alongside the tracks.

"One down," Clint said while watching Terrance roll from the weeds and climb to his feet.

SIXTEEN

Clint kept one hand on the grip of his holstered Colt while reaching out with the other for the passenger car's door. There was a small square window at head level, but he positioned himself away from it so as not to show himself to anyone inside the next car. Closing his eyes for a moment, Clint pictured as much as he could remember about that car in his mind's eye. As far as he could recall, it was only about half full of bench seats and had a small counter where drinks could be purchased. He couldn't remember whether or not there was anyone tending the counter.

"Come on," Nelson said through the door while knocking on it from the other side.

Clint had just been weighing his options in regards to storming through the car to catch up with the other man. His intent was to keep unnecessary gunfire down to a minimum so he'd been hoping to catch Nelson as quickly as possible. For the moment, at least, luck still seemed to be on his side.

"What are you waiting for?" Nelson asked.

"Come here," Clint said in a loud whisper that was just rough enough to do a fairly good job of disguising his voice.

Fortunately, Nelson seemed more annoyed than suspicious when he replied, "Just come on, damn it."

Since he couldn't think of something to say that would bring Nelson to him in a rush without creating the suspicion he was trying to avoid, Clint pulled the door open partway and stepped to one side. All he had to do was wait for a few seconds, his body tensed and ready to jump.

Nelson stuck his head through the barely open doorway, presenting Clint with an opportunity that was far better than he could have hoped for. Grabbing Nelson by the collar, Clint pulled the man partway through and slammed the door on his upper chest.

"How many more of you are on this train?" Clint snarled.

"Who the hell are you?"

Opening the door a bit, Clint slammed it again a little harder. "Answer my question!"

"Where's Terrance?"

"Not on this train any longer." Clint was about to ask his question one more time when he saw Nelson reaching for the pistol at his side. If not for the man he knew to be in the livery, Clint would have pulled Nelson out of the car to deal with him. Instead, he opened the door and shoved Nelson into the passenger car so he could keep some distance between him and Jack Mancuso.

The young woman standing behind the drink counter was first to react at the sight of them. She yelped and jumped back until her back hit the wall behind her. Just over half a dozen passengers were scattered among the seats in the front half of the car. They scattered while making surprised sounds of their own as Clint and Nelson moved toward them.

For the first several paces, Nelson was too surprised to do much of anything. Being slammed between a door and its frame had also squeezed some of the breath from his lungs, which bought Clint a few more seconds to do what he pleased. Clint used that time to keep Nelson moving through the passenger car all the way to the opposite end from where they'd started. Just as Nelson was regaining some of his composure, his back was slammed against another door.

"You pretend like you don't know my face and I'll put you through a window," Clint promised. "Now tell me how many of you are here."

"Kiss my ass."

Clint slammed Nelson against the door one more time. Although he made a solid impact with the other man's body, he lit a fire under Nelson that put him in a fighting mood. Nelson grabbed hold of Clint's wrists and forced him to pull his hands away from him. Once he'd bought himself a small amount of breathing room, Nelson drove a knee into Clint's midsection.

While Clint had tensed his stomach in time to absorb some of the impact, the knee that thumped against his gut still took its toll. Dull pain flowed through his abdomen, robbing him of his next breath. Clint easily slipped his wrists out of Nelson's grasp, but not before Nelson snapped his hands forward to grab both sides of Clint's head.

The next thing Clint saw was Nelson's face driving straight toward him.

After that Clint felt Nelson's forehead pounding against the ridge of his brow. The head butt seemed to cause almost as much pain to Nelson as it did to Clint, but Nelson was too worked up to let that slow him down.

"You like that?" Nelson snarled through the blood that flowed from the cut he'd just opened in his own forehead. "You want some more?"

Clint wasn't about to waste any time with words. His mind was filled only with the things necessary to bring this fight to a swift end. Preferring not to fire a gun among so many innocents, he reached for the door handle directly behind Nelson.

Having gained some momentum in the brawl, Nelson pounded a series of quick hooking punches to Clint's ribs and stomach. Clint tensed his muscles and gritted his teeth, accepting the punishment so he could keep both hands free to open the door the rest of the way. Once that was done, he lowered his shoulder and dug in with both feet to push Nelson out of the car.

Wind blasted them from both sides as they stepped onto the short balcony connecting the two passenger cars. Now that he'd taken the fight to the spot of his choosing, Clint unleashed a few punches of his own. The first few were simply to throw Nelson from the brutal rhythm of his fists tattooing Clint's torso. When Nelson took a step back, Clint put some muscle behind a pair of punches aimed at the other man's head.

Nelson took the punches admirably, not because he was caught unaware but because he wanted to keep Clint in close. His hand dropped to the holster at his hip where he grabbed a pistol and brought it up. The instant it cleared leather, the gun was halted as the hand holding it was stopped cold.

Clint took hold of Nelson's wrist with the speed of a trap clamping shut around an unsuspecting rat. As the sound of the hammer cocking back crackled through the air, Clint forced the gun's barrel away from him. When the pistol went off, Clint could feel the sparks against his side as a round burned past him to sail away from the train.

"It's just the three of you here," Clint said. "Otherwise you would've had some help by now, wouldn't you?"

Nelson bared his teeth as he matched his strength against Clint's in a struggle to point his pistol at its target.

"Or maybe you were just cut loose," Clint continued. "Tossed to the wolves just to make things easier for your boss."

"Go to hell, asshole," Nelson said.

"Why bother protecting them? Tell me..." Clint could no longer worry about what he wanted to say because Nelson had found his second wind and was putting it to use.

An animal's grunt came from Nelson's throat as he inched his pistol toward Clint's head. Beads of sweat rolled down his face, but he was making steady progress toward his deadly goal. "I'm not gonna tell you a damn thing," he said.

"Actually," Clint replied, "I don't need you to." And with that, Clint dropped to one knee while bringing Nelson's arm along with him. He used Nelson's momentum and diverted it to bend the other man's elbow at a painful angle. From his lower position, Clint reached straight down to grab one of Nelson's legs, pulled it out from under him, and flipped it up as he stood up again.

Nelson barely touched the railing as he flipped over it and landed on a slope that led down to a clear blue pond.

"That's two," Clint said. Before he could get too happy with himself, Clint heard the squeal of brakes being applied to the train's wheels and the entire car shuddered beneath him.

SEVENTEEN

The pond was still in sight when the train came to a stop. Clint leaned over the railing to get a better look at it, but couldn't see Nelson any longer. That didn't concern him as much as the fact that there was at least one other man on the train that needed to be dealt with. Clint turned around and stepped into the passenger car he and Nelson had passed through not too long ago.

"You there!" a man wearing a three-piece gray suit said. He stood in the center of the aisle running down the middle of the car, hands on hips and jacket opened to display a finely tooled holster that looked as if it had just been purchased. He was chomping on an unlit stogie and wearing a bowler hat. "Surrender your weapon."

Clint paid him no mind as he continued to approach. Everyone else in that car had the right idea by stepping back and giving him room to pass. The man in the gray suit, however, stood his ground.

"I'm a guard for the railroad," the man in gray announced. "And I have the authority to..." When Clint shoved past him without a word, he added, "Hey, what the--You will not ignore me, Mister!"

Clint stopped, turned toward him, eyed him briefly, then turned back again and continued his walk to the back end of the car.

When he got to the stock car, Clint stopped. One hand was on his gun and the other rested upon the handle of the door in front of him. Before, he'd been reluctant to enter the stock car because he'd been outnumbered. Now that he'd thinned out the gunmen's ranks, he was more confident that he could end the fight without a lot of bloodshed.

Suddenly the door behind him opened and the man in gray stepped outside, wheezing as if he'd run all the way from the engine. "I want some answers, Mister."

All it took for Clint to stop him from saying another word was to shoot a glare in his direction. The man in gray scowled back at him, but held his tongue for the moment. Turning his attention back to the stock car's door, Clint pulled it open and waited without stepping through.

No shots exploded from the car. In fact, the only sound Clint heard was the shifting of a few hooves against the floor boards. Not allowing himself to be lulled by the silence, Clint stepped into the doorway and entered the car.

As he walked down the middle of the car, he checked the stalls one by one. Some were empty. Eclipse was in one. The rest were filled with other passengers' horses. Before he got to the end of the row, a shrill squeak drifted through the air. Clint picked up his pace without opening himself to an attack from either side. There wasn't much of the car left to walk, but he wasn't about to make a stupid mistake.

"Dammit," he said when he saw the door at the end of the car swing open. He kicked the door so it swung all the way out before stepping outside.

By this point, the man in gray had regained some of his backbone. "Where is that other fellow you were fighting with?" he asked. "What was your quarrel with him?"

"He's gone," Clint sighed.

"Obviously."

Stepping to the edge of the balcony between the stock car and the caboose, Clint gazed out at the surrounding terrain. The only movement to be found was the slow swaying of tree branches and tall grass in the wind.

The man in gray propped both hands on his hips, took the unlit stogie from his mouth, and let out a sigh. "Looks like your accomplices got away, huh?"

"Will you just do me a favor and shut the hell up," Clint replied.

EIGHTEEN

In less than half an hour, the train was moving again. The passengers were settled back into their seats and all that remained from the confrontation between Clint and the gunmen was an excited murmur rippling through the passenger cars. As he walked through those cars on his way to the sleeper, Clint received several pensive stares along with some enthusiastic pats on the back from his fellow travelers.

He responded to both with nothing more than a quick glance or an even quicker nod. It wasn't a long walk to the door to the compartment where Selma was waiting, but Clint felt as if he had to walk a mile and a half to get there.

Unable to open the door, Clint knocked and said, "It's me. Open up."

The door opened less than an inch so that one frightened eye could peek through. Almost immediately, the door was opened the rest of the way and Selma rushed to wrap her arms around Clint.

"Oh thank God," she said. "I was so worried."

"No need for that," Clint said as he entered the sleeper compartment and closed the door behind him. "I'm back safe and sound."

"Safe and sound?" She stepped back and hit him on the chest. "When you left this room before, it was

75

through the window!"

"I thought you might appreciate some drama with your train ride."

"Then I heard shooting," she said breathlessly. "And the train stopped. And then men were rushing outside, knocking on the door."

"Someone tried to get in?" Clint asked. "Do you know who they were?"

"I didn't open the door, just like you told me. But I did take a quick look after I heard them walk away, when they thought this compartment was empty." She waved her hand and said, "It was some fellow with a big stomach, a bowler hat, and a mustache."

Recognizing some of that description, Clint asked, "Was he wearing a gray suit?"

"Yes! That was him."

Clint nodded.

"Do you think you can find him?"

"I already met up with him."

"Was he the reason for all the shooting? I mean," Selma added reluctantly, "was he shooting at you? Did you shoot him? I mean..."

Clint stopped her by taking her hands in his and looking her in the eyes. "I know what you mean," he said evenly. "And no. He didn't shoot me and I didn't shoot him. Even if I may have wanted to."

"Oh, no!"

"That last part was a joke," Clint said, even though it was only halfway true. "The man in the gray suit works for the railroad. He gets paid to sit on his ass and keep the passengers in line. This time around, he was more interested in sitting instead of anything else. He didn't even announce his presence until after the shooting was over."

76

"So what was the shooting about?" Selma asked.

"I found some of those men that threatened you," Clint told her. "And, as you might have guessed from the shooting, they found me as well."

She pulled her hands away from his grasp so she could cover her mouth and stare at him through wide eyes.

Clint started to step back but he took her by the shoulders and continued to meet her frightened gaze. "It's all right. Look at me. I'm all right."

"You're filthy and scratched up."

For a second, Clint wasn't sure what she was talking about. Then he took a quick look at his hands and the front of his shirt and pants to find that she was correct. "Oh, that. I was climbing around the outside of the train, remember?"

Selma nodded.

"The rest came in the scuffle." Clint let her go and took a step back from her. Spreading his arms to either side, he smiled and said, "It's nothing serious. See?"

She looked him up and down, lowering her hands and letting out a relieved sigh. When she nodded again, it was different from the last time in that her neck didn't seem like a joint that was badly in need of oil. "So, did you kill those men?" she asked in a vaguely trembling voice.

Clint considered lying to her, if only to ease her nerves for the moment. If those three did survive and did decide they wanted to keep coming, there would be time for the truth later. Unfortunately, one hard lesson that Clint had learned a long time ago was that it was never a good idea to set the truth aside.

"I didn't kill them," he told her. "I just wanted to get them off the train. Of course, I didn't do that in a very

77

gentle way, but I doubt the tumble killed them. I've been thrown from a few moving trains myself and can tell you it doesn't have to be fatal."

"But they're gone? All of them?"

"For now. I was hoping to meet up with at least one of them, but when the train stopped, he must've hopped off. With me, the man in the gray suit, and everyone else gawking out their windows while we were stopped, I seriously doubt anyone could have climbed back on again before we got moving. Even so, I'd still like you to stay in here until we reach the station."

Selma smiled, pressed her hands against Clint's shoulders and shoved him back. "You mean we'll stay in here."

"Right."

Now that Clint's back was against the door, he found himself sandwiched between it and Selma. "You don't exactly seem frightened anymore," he said.

"I'm not. Not with you, here."

"We really should stay on our guard, just in case there are any more of those men on this train."

"They won't get us in here," Selma said while leaning in closer to him. "And even if they did, you could take care of them."

"We don't want them getting inside."

Propping one foot against the door so it brushed against Clint's hip, Selma said, "Then I should press up against it real hard to block it."

"Sounds like a plan," Clint said as he slid one hand under her skirts and up along her thigh.

NINETEEN

When Selma kissed him, Clint felt the heat of her breath along with the soft wetness of her tongue slipping into his mouth. She pressed her lips against his with just as much urgency as she pulled at his belt buckle to loosen his jeans. He helped her a bit by removing his holster and dropping it to the floor, only to return his hands straight back to her body. The room was small enough that the gun would always be within his reach.

He could feel the taut muscles beneath her skin as he ran one palm along her thigh while using the other hand to reach around and cup her backside. As their kiss became longer and more intense, he moved his hand from her buttocks to the hot spot between her legs. She was slick and damp there. When Clint worked his fingertips within the thatch of hair between her thighs, he could hear Selma's breath catch in the back of her throat.

Clint felt an urgency within his body as well. It made him grab her buttocks in both hands, lift her slightly and turn her around so she was suddenly the one with her back against the door. Her eyes grew wide on impact and she pushed her next breath out with eager anticipation. Selma lowered one foot to the floor for balance and wrapped her other leg around Clint's lower body to draw him in closer.

As he moved his hands beneath her skirts to feel the smooth curves of her hips, Clint tasted the flesh of her neck by licking her skin and occasionally biting just hard enough to make Selma's pulse race. Their hands moved with an agenda of their own, stripping just enough clothes from the other's body to suit their purpose. When Clint's erection found the wet lips of her pussy, they both stopped for a moment to savor it.

That moment passed quickly and Clint drove all the way inside of her with one thrust of his hips.

"Jesus," Selma said as she arched her back and pressed the back of her head against the door. When Clint began pumping in and out of her, she gripped his shoulders hard enough to dig her fingernails into his flesh.

Every time Clint entered her, he pulled her lower body in close so he could enter her as deeply as possible. He lingered for a second or two before easing out and pushing back in again. Every time, she was a little wetter than the last and she gripped him as if she didn't want to let him go.

Soon, his instincts took over and his body took on a more powerful rhythm. Every time he buried his cock between her legs, Selma's body thumped against the door and she let out a throaty, satisfied grunt. For a short while, those noises followed one after another until Clint's breathing became labored as well. He wasn't tired so much as he was becoming drained from the process of straining with nearly every muscle in his body.

"Here," Selma said as she stood on both feet again. "Let me."

At first, Clint thought she was referring to the way she reached down with one hand to stroke his cock. His rigid pole was still wet from her and Selma's fingers moved up and down along its length with ease. But she only massaged him for a few moments before letting him go and turning her back to him. She used one hand to gather her skirts and keep them hiked up while pushing her other hand flat against the door. Touching her cheek against the door as well, she looked over her shoulder and waited.

Clint wasn't about to make her wait more than a few seconds as he admired the view of her lower back sloping smoothly to the plumpness of her ass. Then he guided his hard cock between her legs so he could feel the wetness there without slipping between her thin pink lips.

Clawing at the wall like a cat, Selma leaned back and took a wider stance to accept him. "Don't make me wait for it," she said. "Please."

Tightening his grip, Clint pushed inside of her and drove all the way until he was as deep as he could go. Selma tossed her hair back while letting out a trembling moan. Like the engine pulling the train around them, Clint built up steam until he was pumping in and out of her in long, powerful movements. Every time he entered her, he sent a quake through Selma's body and when he pulled out again, he could feel her pussy gripping him to keep him from getting away.

He drove into her again and again, without even realizing that Selma was pushing hard enough against the door to make the hinges creak. Normally, Clint would have heard the footsteps approaching from the hallway outside, but he was too preoccupied to notice until they stopped directly in front of the door separating Selma from the rest of the passengers.

"Everything all right in there?" the conductor asked while knocking gently.

"Yes," Selma replied breathlessly. "Fine. Just fine."

"You certain about that?"

Clint smirked. Unable to help himself, he pushed slowly into her while pulling Selma's hips toward him.

"Y--yes," she sighed as every inch of his rigid cock filled her. "Yes. Oh, yes!"

"All right then," the conductor replied before walking away in nice, easy steps.

TWENTY

"You all right?"

Jack Mancuso stood alongside the railroad tracks, rubbing his knee when he heard the gravelly voice ask that question. The man who'd asked it was a little shorter than average height and had a wide build as if his stocky body had somehow been flattened into an awkward oval shape. Thick brown hair sprouted from his head to frame a gnarled face covered in darker brown whiskers. Despite his natural ugliness, the stranger had a certain friendliness about him.

Matching the stranger's concerned expression with a tired smile, Mancuso replied, "I'm all right. A little battered but all right."

"Anything I can do for ya?"

"Do you have a horse?"

The stranger nodded and showed Mancuso a wide smile that was missing several teeth. "I sure do. You need a ride into town?"

"That would be nice."

"Come along with me," the stranger said as he hooked a thick arm up and around in a wave. "The old girl's not too far. Name's Mick, by the way."

"I'm Jack."

"Pleased to meet you, Jack. You mind if I ask what brings you all the way out in the middle of this here

83

field?"

It only took a few steps for Mancuso to get his legs moving at a normal pace. His jeans were torn and bloody and his shirt was covered in dirt and ripped in several places. Looking down at his ragged clothes, he chuckled once and said, "It's a long story."

"I imagine. Judging by the state you're in, my guess was that you were tossed off'a that train."

"Is that so?"

Mick laughed and kept walking with a limp that had obviously been with him for quite a while. "If I hadn't seen more'n my own share of hard times, I wouldn't be able to think of many other ways for you to wind up like that."

"How many can you think of?"

Holding up a gnarled hand, Mick said, "Could'a been dumped off the back of a wagon by a crazy woman. Maybe you escaped a lynch mob. Might be that you fell off'a your horse and rolled down a hill. Plenty of common type things like that without me havin' to get too creative."

"Those weren't your creative guesses?" Mancuso asked.

Mick used the same hand to tap his temple while turning to look at Mancuso. "I got a complicated mind."

Nodding his agreement to that, Mancuso asked, "So what is it that brings you out here? Something creative?"

"Not hardly. I was riding into town, watching the train chug along and saw it come to a stop, brakes screaming like a bag of skinned and salted cats."

"Skinned and salted, huh? You do have a complicated mind, my friend."

"That's one word for it," Mick replied. "So which is it? Was I close on any of my guesses?"

"Actually you were right on the first guess."

"Ha! You fell off the train?"

When Mancuso drew his pistol, he was close enough to shove it directly into Mick's ample belly before pulling the trigger. The gun made a few muffled thumps, lifting Mick off his feet each time. The last one was a bit louder since it blew a large hole through Mick's back.

The horse that Mancuso had spotted tied to some trees nearby stirred slightly, surprised a bit by the gunshots. Mancuso calmed it with a few kind words and a gentle pat on the nose before climbing into its saddle and snapping the reins. He left Mick behind, twitching in the dirt, so he could ride back along the tracks to find what was left of his partners.

TWENTY-ONE

For most of the rest of the ride, Clint stayed in the compartment with Selma. A large part of that was due to her being so fired up after the excitement she'd partly witnessed and another part was to avoid the man in the gray suit. Every now and then, the railroad man could be heard stomping up and down the hall running the length of the passenger car but Clint ignored him with admirable resolve.

The only time Clint ventured out of the sleeper compartment was to hurry into another car for something to drink before scurrying right back to Selma's open arms and legs. Perhaps it was just the excitement or maybe it was the motion of the train as well, but her enthusiasm didn't wane. A more conceited man might have thought it was his own charms that kept Selma's blood boiling throughout the entire ride. The fact of the matter was that Clint simply didn't have much time to ask too many questions. He was kept too busy to care about such things as why's and how come's.

Clint's toes were still curled after Selma's most recent efforts when she swatted him on the shoulder and said, "We're here! We're here! Come on."

"All right," he said wearily. "Get your bags."

"You're not going to help me with them?"

"You're the one who had to pack so much for what's supposed to be a short trip," he reminded her. "If you don't have the good sense to travel lightly, then you're the one that should have to pay the price."

A few minutes later, Selma stepped off the train. Clint wasn't far behind her, holding a bag in each hand and a smaller one tucked under one arm. The platform sported a fresh coat of paint, which Clint could see very well since there was only one other person standing on it with them.

"Where is everybody?" he asked while looking around. He'd been to San Francisco before, and this looked strange.

"Who were you expecting? A welcome committee? I thought we weren't trying to draw attention to ourselves."

"I wasn't expecting a committee." He looked around. "I was just expecting more people than this. I mean, San Francisco is a big place."

"You're right," Selma said in a voice that she might also use when speaking to a slow-witted child. "San Francisco is a mighty big place. This just isn't San Francisco."

"It's not?"

"No."

"I thought that's where we were headed!"

"We were headed to my father's spread which is just outside of San Francisco," she explained. "His company is based out of there, but he lives here."

Clint looked around again, focusing on the signs posted about instead of the people that weren't filling the platform. "And here is...Ola Blanca?" he asked, reading the words painted underneath the phrase "Welcome to".

Patting him on the arm, she said, "That's right. You can read. Very good."

"All right," Clint grunted. "That's enough of the smart talk. It would've been nice to know this ahead of time is all I'm saying."

"I did tell you we'd be departing here. I even mentioned it by name."

"When?"

"Remember when you were stretching your back after we..."

"Oh yeah," Clint replied fondly. "I might not have been paying full attention."

"I bet. And you didn't bother reading the tickets I bought either?"

"I just assumed they said..." Stopping himself right there, Clint said, "You know what? It doesn't matter. We're here. This is where we're supposed to be. The stock car is being unloaded right now, so I'm just going to go over there and fetch my horse."

"Sounds like a good idea." Selma found a small bench nearby and sat down. Looking up at Clint while batting her eyelashes daintily, she asked, "You do remember which horse is yours, right?"

Clint had a response to that, but it wasn't fit for mixed company. Even though there weren't enough other people on that platform to be considered any sort of company, he kept his voice down to a grumble as he walked to a ramp leading into the livery car. The liveryman who led Eclipse out wasn't familiar to Clint in the slightest.

"Where's the other man?" Clint asked.

Wincing, the fellow replied, "What other man?"

"Oh, that's right!" Clint said. "I knocked him off the train. That means you're probably the one who let him on in the first place."

"No! I swear! I don't know any of that. All that I know is that..."

"Save it," Clint snapped, not wanting to hear whatever script the other man had surely memorized. It always boiled down to the same thing anyhow.

Some men can be bought.

Most men...

Other men do the buying.

Clint didn't need to interrogate anyone to know which he was looking at. He also wasn't interested in doing the railroad's job by punishing the guilty party working for them. He took some degree of comfort from the sight of the man in the gray suit leaning against the back wall of the livery car watching the worker like a hawk.

"Have a good stay, Mister Adams," the man in gray said as he tapped his finger against the brim of his bowler hat and smiled around his unlit cigar.

The talk he'd had with the railroad man after the scuffle with Mancuso and the other two had been short and uneventful. The man in gray was simply going through the motions of what he thought someone in his position should do and nothing more. Clint had already had his fill of men like that and was surely at his limit with this one in particular so he answered back with nothing more than an off-handed wave.

Eclipse let out a huffing breath and shook his head.

"If you're saying you'd rather be in San Francisco right now," Clint said under his breath, "I'm inclined to agree with you."

TWENTY-TWO

The town of Ola Blanca was close enough to see from the station, but too far away for Clint and Selma to walk there. After the time spent on the train, Clint was more than happy to climb into the saddle and ride for a short stretch. Eclipse was even happier and would have been perfectly content to gallop straight on through town and onward to the great Pacific coastline.

"Are we there yet?" Selma asked. With her arms wrapped around Clint's midsection and squeezing the stuffing out of him, it was clear that she wasn't exactly happy for the race into town.

"Just about," Clint replied. "If you open your eyes, you'd see for yourself."

"That's quite all right. I think I'll keep them closed for a while longer."

"Suit yourself."

They rode the rest of the way without any more conversation. It was a welcome respite, even if it only lasted for less than half an hour. By the end of that time, Clint pulled back on the reins and slowed Eclipse to a quick walk. Selma's grip around him loosened somewhat and she began to shift in the saddle behind him.

"Oh, this is more like it," she sighed gratefully. "It's been too long."

"How long has it been?" Clint asked.

"Six months or so," she said. "Actually, I've passed through here on occasion in that time, but never stayed for more than half a day. It feels good to know I'll be staying home for a while."

"That depends."

"On what?"

Not wanting to be the one to douse her good spirits, Clint held his tongue until Selma reminded herself of the circumstances of their visit.

It didn't take long.

"Oh," she said. "Right. There might be more men coming for me."

"From what you've told me so far, Selma," he said to her, "it seems to me there will definitely be more men coming after you."

While Clint didn't want to incite any panic in Selma's mind, he also wanted to make sure she had a firm grasp of what was happening. Because if either one of them wasn't clear this far along, there would be some bigger problems in the near future.

"You're right," she said. "I should keep my focus on the danger at hand. Thank you for reminding me." She pressed her cheek against his back.

Even though he was glad to hear her say that, Clint couldn't help but feel like an ass for draining the cheer from her tone in such a short amount of time. "It's going to be all right," he assured her. "The whole reason I'm here is to help with that."

"Right!" Selma said, brightening up almost immediately. "And you already have helped! For all we know, this whole mess may be over after what you did on that train." Once again, she cinched her grip around his midsection and followed up by laying her head on the back of Clint's shoulder. "Everything is going to be just fine."

"Sure," he said.

There was the lackadaisical tone that Clint had been trying to avoid in the first place. Knowing there was no reason in going around that particular circle again, he let her continue to think killers like Jack Mancuso and the men riding with him could give up so easily.

At least that way he could enjoy the rest of his ride into town in peace.

TWENTY-THREE

Mancuso didn't have to ride for long before he met up with one of his partners. What surprised him was which partner he found first.

"Where's Nelson?" he asked.

Terrance rode an old gray mare that was missing an ear. Judging by the tattered flaps of skin protruding from the girl's head, the ear had either been shot or chewed off. Either way, the mare took almost as little notice of it as she did of the man riding on her back. Terrance himself wore a wide grin as he waved toward Mancuso and asked, "He ain't with you?"

"Does it look like he's with me?"

Terrance stood in his stirrups and made a show of looking past Mancuso. "No," he said while settling back onto his horse's back. "Guess not."

"So I take it you haven't seen him."

"That's right. I was too busy falling off a train."

"I wouldn't be so proud of that if'n I was you," Mancuso snarled.

Terrance rode up to get beside Mancuso. "Not exactly proud. I took a few bumps along the way, but it could've been a whole lot worse. What did you hear about Nelson?"

"He got tossed as well."

"I say we look for him for a short while and then get on with the job. Not like we need him anyway, right?"

Mancuso answered with only a grunt before snapping his reins and continuing along the tracks.

***

Less than a mile away, Mancuso spotted a single figure stumbling down the middle of the tracks. From a distance, the man could have been any vagrant using the tracks as a path from one town to another. But he suspected that wasn't just another vagrant and in short order, that suspicion was confirmed.

For a while, it seemed as though the figure hadn't even spotted the two horses headed toward him. When he did, he pulled his gun from its holster and glared intently at the other two men.

Mancuso rode straight up to him and asked, "What the hell do you intend on doing with that?"

"Jack?" the figure asked.

"Course it's me, Nelson. Who else would waste a second of their time looking for you?"

"Both of you got tossed, then?"

"Looks that way," Terrance said. "But at least the two of us managed to find ourselves a horse."

"Go fuck yourself, asshole!" Nelson hollered as he holstered his gun. Once Terrance started laughing loudly enough for it to echo in every direction, he skinned the pistol again real quick.

"Both of you give it a rest!" Mancuso roared. "It ain't as if either of you two got a damn thing to be proud of!"

Turning his face toward Mancuso, Nelson said, "Seems that would apply to all three of us, seeing as how you're off that train as well."

Mancuso didn't say a word until he'd ridden to within several paces of where Nelson was standing. He didn't take his eyes off of the other man for one second of that time, however, which made Nelson increasingly less comfortable in his position. Pulling back hard on his reins, Mancuso said, "Unlike the two of you, I climbed down from that train of my own accord. I wasn't tossed like a sack of shit over the side."

Neither of the other men had much of anything to say to that.

In a humbler tone of voice, Nelson asked, "What happened?"

"Adams almost got exactly what he was after," Mancuso replied. "That's what happened. And once the railroad men got too nervous from all the noise, they stopped the train to do a proper search. Since tearing through all those men would've been more trouble than it was worth, I decided to disembark."

"Well, that's a much more graceful exit than we got," Terrance said through a nervous chuckle. As he spoke, his eyes darted to Mancuso's hand that hovered above his pistol. "We appreciate you coming back for us."

"You should be more appreciative that I don't bury both of you right here on this spot."

"Why would you do that?"

"Because you're about as useless as a limp prick in a whorehouse!" Mancuso raged.

Nelson, tired and battered as he was, had enough wherewithal to avert his eyes and lower his head a bit. Standing like a coyote before the biggest dog in the pack, he said, "You're right, Jack. We got caught off guard. It won't happen again."

"You're goddamn right about that."

"So what now, Boss?" Terrance asked in a voice that was a bit too chipper for Mancuso's liking. When he saw the fire in Mancuso's eyes as he glared at him, Terrance took a page from Nelson's book and cowed slightly. "I mean...what should we do now, do you think?"

Mancuso sighed, becoming both more patient and more aggravated at the same time. The only thing that tempered his mood was the fatigue that had soaked into the bones of all three men after their exits from the train. "We go along with the plan as it was," he said. "The schedule might be thrown off a bit, but there's no reason to think we can't proceed."

"Hell yes!" Almost immediately, Terrance regained his composure and said, "That's right, sir."

"Cut the bullshit," Mancuso said. "Don't be worried about kissing my ass and be more worried with doing your damn part in all of this."

Not quite sure what to say, Terrance merely nodded.

"You know we're lucky to be alive," Nelson said. Unlike the last time he was on the receiving end of Mancuso's angry stare, he didn't turn away. Also unlike the previous time, Mancuso didn't seem quite as ready to tear another man's head off. Instead, there was an understanding between the two that was acknowledged by a slow nod from Nelson. "That wasn't just some man with a gun," he said. "That was Clint Adams."

"I know," Mancuso replied.

"So?" Terrance asked. Before he was slapped down, he quickly added, "What I mean is what difference does it make who it is? We knew men were going to be called on to hunt us down. That's how it is for every job. The point is that we can do this no matter who it is that's after us."

"He's right," Mancuso said.

Although he wasn't about to say as much himself, Nelson didn't dispute the statement either.

Even so, Terrance nodded as though he had a whole choir singing his praises. "Yeah. That's right. I heard of Clint Adams, too. In fact, we may even be better off if Adams thinks he got rid of one or two of us today. Should give us the evidence of surprise."

"What?" Nelson snapped.

"You know. The evidence of surprise."

"Element. Element of surprise."

"Whichever," Terrance said with a dismissing wave. "We got it, sure enough."

Now, neither of the other two men wanted to admit that Terrance had a point.

TWENTY-FOUR

hen Clint climbed down from his saddle, he was ready to get off his feet for a spell. Helping Selma down from Eclipse's back, he quickly realized that she didn't feel the same. In fact, she had more energy than ever once her feet touched the ground in front of the long house built on the southern edge of town. Without so much as a backward glance, she dashed away from him and headed straight for the front door.

Clint took Eclipse's reins and dropped them to the ground. The horse wouldn't move until he came back for him. "Take your rests when you can get 'em," Clint said. "You should know just as well as I do that they don't come as often as we'd like them to."

"Ain't that the truth."

Clint turned toward the sound of the voice. It hadn't surprised him, since he'd heard the footsteps preceding it. And since those steps had clomped against the boards of the nearby porch before crunching against the dirt, he figured the man who'd spoken hadn't been trying to sneak up on him.

That man was the same height as Clint and had the solid build of someone who'd been taking it easy after several years of hard work. His skin was tanned from the sun and toughened by the elements, which made his thick mane of hair seem even lighter in comparison.

The smile he showed to Clint seemed genuine enough, however, which was a good start.

"I'm Derrick Coates," the man said.

"Clint Adams."

"Welcome to my home, Clint Adams," Coates greeted. "I take it you're the one responsible for bringing my daughter home to me?"

"I am."

"Then I don't know whether I should shake your hand or punch you in the face."

Clint smirked. "If I didn't know your situation, I might be offended by that."

"And, to be honest, if it wasn't for my situation, I would never have said something like that to a man I've got no quarrel with." Extending a hand covered in leathery skin, Derrick said, "You have every right to be offended, sir. My apologies."

Clint shook his hand. "No need for apologies and no need to call me sir. Clint will do just fine."

"All right, then. Now this is a better start."

Derrick Coates' grip was solid and strong as an ox, just what Clint would have expected from a man who'd built up a company from one storefront and a partial interest in a seafaring boat to an entire company with at least a hundred people on its payroll.

"Daddy!" Selma called out from nearby. "Did you meet Clint?"

"That I did, sweet pea," Coates said. "He's right here with me."

"Are you trying to scare him?"

When Clint raised an eyebrow, Coates shook his head and told him, "She's always had this crazy notion that I tried to scare the daylights out of any of the boys who looked at her sideways."

"Did you?" Clint asked.

"Well, maybe a little. If you had daughters, you'd understand."

"I think I can imagine."

"Well, that one was a handful," Coates said, "let me tell you."

"Now, that," Clint said, "is something I don't need to imagine."

Mister Coates looked at Clint with a mix of suspicion and dread as if he could read some of the thoughts drifting through Clint's mind. On the off chance he was tipping his hand a bit too much, Clint cleared the fond memories from his mind and stepped back over to Eclipse.

"Will I be staying here tonight or should I find a hotel in town?" Clint asked.

Although he opened his mouth to respond, Coates didn't get a word out before his daughter chimed in. "What's he telling you?" she asked while sticking her head out from one of the house's front windows. "Did he tell you to leave?"

"No," Clint said.

"Not yet anyway," Coates added, giving him a good look at the kind of menace he must have shown to so many of Selma's other would be suitors. As far as mean glares went, it wasn't half bad.

Raising his hands as if he was surrendering at gunpoint, Clint explained, "I'm only here to help."

Slowly, Coates relaxed the intensity in his eyes. That expression melted directly into a much warmer smile. "My daughter seems to trust you, so that buys you a stay of execution. Come on in," he said while leading the way to the house, "and I'll buy you a drink."

Clint followed along, chuckling at the joke regarding execution. At least, he thought it was a joke.

TWENTY-FIVE

errick Coates' office was barely more than a large closet stuffed with bookshelves and a small liquor cabinet. The only reason it could be called an office at all was because of the small roll top desk situated against one wall directly beneath a rectangular window looking out on the western edge of his property. The surface of the desk was covered in folded papers, opened envelopes, a letter opener, some fountain pens, and two ink wells. Coates ignored the desk completely and instead walked straight over to the liquor cabinet.

"All right, Mister Adams," he said while opening the top of the waist high cabinet to retrieve a glass and a bottle of whiskey. "Tell me your intentions toward my daughter."

"Uhhhhhh..."

Even if Clint may have figured the other man was joking, he didn't feel completely relieved until he saw the other man break the stern countenance he'd put on while pouring the whiskey from its bottle into a glass. By the time he handed over the drink to Clint, Coates was grinning widely again.

"Come on, Clint," he said. "This can't be the first time you've heard someone say those words to you."

"It isn't," Clint admitted. "But it's never easy when I do."

"And I'm sure it's never very amusing, either," Coates said. "Still, it's a good way for a man like me to see a man like you squirm."

Clint took the glass from Coates and sipped the whiskey. There was no expensive label on the bottle, but the liquor within was distinctly flavorful. It being Coates' selection told Clint that Coates was more concerned with a good drink instead of trying to impress his guest by flashing his money around.

"You like it?" Coates asked. "I got a few bottles from one of my shipments that came all the way from Scotland."

It was a simple statement of fact, which allowed Clint to hang on to his impression that Coates wasn't much concerned with appearances.

"I prefer beer," Clint said, "but a whiskey like this is nothing to pass up."

"I agree." Pouring himself some more he could take a drink, Coates turned to walk a few steps across the room and stand in front of the window. "I'm guessing you came here for a job."

"I came here because I heard about the threat made to your company as well as to your family."

"Exactly," Coates said. "And since you're here in that regard, I would imagine you're looking to be hired on as protection."

"I didn't come here for money, Mister Coates."

Turning back around, Coates faced Clint with a perplexed expression. "What then? You just wanted to help?"

"Well, nothing's for nothing, but let's say it's not the main reason I'm here."

"See, now that's exactly the sort of thing that makes a face to face meeting like this so important. If I'd read this in a telegram or letter, or even had someone tell me what you'd just said, I'd never believe it."

"Why not?" Clint asked.

"Because nobody does anything for free," Coates replied without missing a beat.

"Nobody?"

"Let's just say the number is so small that it's damn near insignificant."

Clint raised his glass. "On that, Mister Coates, we can agree."

After finishing the rest of the whiskey he'd poured for himself, Coates held on to his glass and said, "But you're part of that insignificant number, aren't you?"

"I wouldn't exactly like to think of it in those words," Clint said with a wince.

"Not that you're insignificant," Coates assured him. "Just that you're part of that slim number of men who truly say what they mean. I've gotten a long ways by being able to size men up fairly quickly and everything in my gut tells me that you mean what you just told me about wanting to help."

"I'd be surprised if I was your only line of defense in that regard."

"Would you?"

"You're a man of means, Mister Coates," Clint said. "A man with a family. I doubt you'd take a threat like this very lightly."

"A man in my spot gets plenty of threats from those who want some of what he's got," Derrick said. "But there's already been blood spilled by these particular men and so no, I'm not taking this threat very lightly."

"Then why don't you already have someone guarding your interests? More specifically," Clint added, waving his hand, "this house?"

"I'm not one of these businessmen who surround themselves with hired hands. I don't need a bunch of strangers doing my work. Granted, I do have men on my payroll, but not to protect my home. That's my job and mine alone and it would be wise not to doubt I can do it."

"I'm not doubting that," Clint said. "And I would never presume to accuse a man of not being able to protect his own. That job becomes a lot harder once that man's interests expand to include an entire company."

Coates let out a sigh while turning back around to face the window. "You're right about that. It's a shame, too. I've heard a few things about you, Adams, but not a lot beyond rumors and some wild stories. Have you ever been involved in a business venture?"

"Nothing as large as Coates Shipping, but yeah. I've dabbled in a few investments."

"It takes a whole lot of fire in a man's belly to get something like that up and running. Funny thing is that same fire makes it awfully hard to sit still and tend to the day to day tasks."

"Now that," Clint said, "is definitely something I understand."

Coates crossed the little room to grab the whiskey bottle and hold it for Clint to see. When he got a nod, he filled both glasses again. "You've already done plenty just by bringing Selma back home. If you'd still want to do more to protect my family, I'd be plenty appreciative."

"I've got a few ideas."

TWENTY-SIX

At the end of the day, Clint felt as if he'd been put through a wringer by Derrick Coates. It wasn't enough to put a limp in his step, but he certainly didn't have much wind left in his sails as he stepped through the door of Granny's Boarding House on Main Street. As much as he wanted to scoff at the name of the place, Clint couldn't deny the warm, inviting smells that made it feel instantly like a home. Now he knew why Coates had told him that was the place to go to eat.

"And you'll find Selma there, too," the man said. "She loves that place."

"Well hello there," said a plump woman in her early seventies wrapped up in a light blue dress, white apron, and a fine layer of flour. "Do you need a room for the night?"

"No, ma'am," Clint replied. "I'm looking for...her."

From the next room, Selma appeared. She wore a different dress than the last time he'd seen her, but the hungry look in her eyes was very familiar.

"There you are, Clint," she said. "I thought you'd left town."

"Not hardly," Clint said while crossing the room to her. "Your father gave me a tour of his building here in town. Or, I should say, one of his buildings here in town."

"Is that what's occupied the two of you all this time?" she asked. "It's been hours since I saw you at my father's house."

"That and some discussion about what my role in the company will be."

She raised her eyebrows and put on an overly impressed expression. "You have a position in the company now? My, my. You seem to be moving up in the world."

"That depends," Clint said as he offered Selma his arm, "on what you thought of my position before I got here."

"I can think of plenty of positions for both of us after we eat."

Clint smiled and nodded. He'd thrown out his last comment already pondering the lewd responses it might bring and Selma hadn't disappointed him. Even with her lack of originality, however, Clint felt a stirring deep down in him when he heard the lusty growl in her voice.

"You two don't mind me," the old woman said as she bustled past Selma and Clint. "I'll just put something together for supper."

"Don't worry about offending her with any of our talk," Selma said with a quick wave at the old woman's back.

"I wasn't worried, but it might be more proper if we mind our manners."

"Proper?" she laughed. "That woman ran whorehouses in eight different towns. Rough towns, mind you. Not the little places where whores didn't need protection." When she leaned in close and lowered her voice, it was obviously not through any sense of propriety. "I'd wager she's got at least one pistol secreted away beneath all those petticoats."

"Sounds like an interesting woman," Clint said.

"My father brought her in to run this place because she could also keep an eye on all the whores in town."

Looking around as if he could see more than the last time he'd cast his eyes in those same directions, Clint asked, "Are girls working out of this boarding house?"

"No," Selma said, "but they're scattered throughout town. They all just work where they like and Margie here sends customers their way."

"How does that work?"

"I don't know. You'd have to ask Margie. She's in complete charge of the whores."

No, that's not necessary," Clint said. "I was just curious."

"Oh, sure," the old woman said, as she stepped past them and nudged Clint with her elbow. "That's what they all say. When you get curious enough, you know where to find me."

While his eyes weren't exactly feasting on the sight of the old girl, Clint's mind couldn't help but wander into some strange directions. He put an end to that with a quick, vigorous shake of his head before following Selma to a table where two glasses of lemonade were already waiting for them.

"So," Selma said as she sat down. "Did my father talk you into staying on for a bit?"

"I doubt there's much of a reason for that," Clint replied. "You're here and Derrick seems more than capable of keeping you safe."

"Didn't he ask you to stay?"

"He made an offer, but it wasn't exactly urgent. He said he could use all the capable hands he could get and that I'd be paid well while I was here."

"Sounds good," she said with a nod.

"I might sign on with him for a while, but I'm not needed here as much as I am in San Francisco."

She was still nodding for a few seconds as those words sank in. Once she'd finally digested what had just been said, Selma gasped, "Wait. What? San Francisco?"

"Isn't that where most of your father's business is?" he asked.

"Yes, but..."

"Well then, that's probably why he offered me some work there."

"Why would you want to go to San Francisco?" she asked, impatiently.

Clint blinked slowly as though he could barely understand the question. "Haven't you ever been there? It's really quite nice."

Selma's lips pressed together to form a thin line. Her brow furrowed into a series of equally thin lines that made her face look like a sketch that was in the process of being scratched away. "I'd rather you stayed here," she said.

Approaching her so he was close enough to put his hands on her hips, Clint said, "I'm not leaving right away. Let's just enjoy what we've got when we've got it."

Her smile was pretty enough, if more than a little forced. "I guess you're right. But what kind of work did my father offer you?"

"Oh, just some odd jobs here and there," Clint explained. "Why don't I just tell you more about it while we eat? I'm starving."

"Me, too."

"Then let's eat."

TWENTY-SEVEN

Jack Mancuso, Nelson Stamp and Terrance Jordan approached Ola Blanca from the northeast on an old trail that was too broken down for most wagons to use. After roaming the Pacific coastline for the better part of ten years, all three men knew the lay of the land so well that they barely needed sunlight to traverse it.

As he reined his horse to a stop, Mancuso held up a hand to signal for the other two to do the same.

"Aw, don't tell me we're sleeping on the damn ground when there's perfectly good beds that close!" Terrance whined.

"Shut yer hole," Nelson snapped. "If we're to camp tonight, then we'll camp."

"We ain't camping," Mancuso said.

Nelson let out half a breath. "Thank God."

Pointing to one end of town, Mancuso continued, "I'll ride in from the north and Terrance will come in from the east. Nelson, you'll circle around to the south end of town and approach from there."

"Where are we meeting up?" Terrance asked.

"We ain't," Mancuso told him. "At least not right away. We get into town without drawing attention and see what's what."

"Why all the sneaking around?"

"Because Adams is most likely in there along with Lord knows how many men hired by that Coates fella."

Terrance gnawed on some piece of meat that he'd just sucked from between his teeth, formed it into a juicy wad, and spat it onto the ground. "That's what I think of Adams. I'll gladly take another run at him if he's even got the balls to show his face again."

"That's some mighty tough talk comin' from the man that Adams tossed off a train," Nelson chided.

"Hey! He tossed you as well, asshole!"

Before the discussion could get any further out of hand, Mancuso brought his horse around to face them both. "Neither one of you got any room to talk where Adams is concerned. Right now, you just do what I say and be ready to prove yourselves when you get the chance. This has all the makings of a damn easy job and if either of you ruin that, I'll tear off your fucking heads and use the stump as a spittoon. Got it?"

Both other men responded with nods before snapping their reins to ride in their appointed directions. Mancuso watched them for a few seconds before heading toward Ola Blanca, all the while, savoring the thought of splitting the final profits two or even one way instead of three.

TWENTY-EIGHT

Dinner was over fairly quickly. Part of that was because Margie served them two plates of food left over from when she'd cooked for some of her guests a bit earlier in the evening. After taking a few bites, Clint didn't have to wonder why there was so much of the stuff left over. Another reason for the short suppertime was because he didn't have much to tell Selma in regard to his conversation with her father.

"So that's it?" she asked as they left the boarding house. "Daddy just asked you to make some deliveries and ride along with a few wagons?"

"That's right."

"Sound's boring."

"Sometimes that's not such a bad thing," Clint said. "In fact, after the time I had just getting here, I wouldn't mind some boring one bit."

"But still," she sneered. "You don't seem like the sort of man who would enjoy something so tame."

"Tell you what," Clint said as he wrapped an arm around her and pulled Selma close as they walked along the street, "you escort a wagon full of expensive goods through Indian country and then tell me how boring it is."

"Will there be bandits too?"

"Could be."

115

Even though it wasn't a particularly chilly evening, Selma nestled in tight against Clint while resting her head on his shoulder. "Now that sounds exciting enough to get my blood boiling."

Knowing what she was like when her blood ran hot in her veins, Clint said, "Ok. Then there will definitely be bandits. Probably some real tough ones."

"I like the sound of that."

"Most likely they'll be wanted men," Clint added as he straightened his posture and stuck out his chest. "Maybe I'll come back around once I've cashed in the money I get from dragging them back into a jail cell." He wasn't now and had never been a bounty hunter. He was just trying to make sure Selma was good and worried about him.

"Even better!" As she walked, Selma eased a hand down along the front of Clint's body so she could reach between his legs. There weren't many other people to be found on the street, but she was still quick to pull her hand back to a more respectable spot.

"No matter who I find," Clint said, "I'll still have to come through here again."

"You'd better. I'm not through with you just yet, Clint Adams."

"I sincerely hope not."

After a few more steps, they rounded a corner and headed down a busier street. There were a few saloons to be found along with some other places that showed signs of revelry. It was getting too dark to read the signs posted on those buildings, but enough rowdy voices and commotion could be heard for Clint to make a good guess as to what was inside them.

"Please tell me you won't be leaving right away," Selma said.

"I wasn't planning on it. Not for another day or two, anyhow."

"Good, because I've got plans for you."

"You keep talking big like that," Clint said, "but so far that's all it is. We're still just out strolling in the moonlight."

Selma planted her feet and turned on her heels to face him. She placed her hands upon her hips and took an offended tone when she said, "After all the times I've fucked you, you think I'm just talk?"

"What did you just say?"

"Why do you look so shocked? Is the great Clint Adams really a puritan?"

"Puritan?" Clint said. "Is that what you really think of me?"

She shrugged her shoulders and cast her eyes in another direction as if she was suddenly growing weary of the conversation. "Maybe."

Clint clapped his hands together before rubbing them vigorously like a lumberjack that was about to heft his axe. "All right, then. I suppose I'll just have to prove myself."

"And how will you do that?" When he started coming at her, Selma backed away while holding her hands in front of her. "Clint? What are you doing?"

"Proving myself the only way a man knows how. Like a brute. And if you tell me you don't like that, I'll know you're lying."

"Like it?" she asked, unable to hide an excited smirk. "What will you do if you get a hold of me?"

"What do you mean if?"

Clint lunged for her, expecting Selma to hop away. Although she did, the expression on her face suddenly lost all of its playfulness. "What's the matter?" he asked.

His question was still drifting through the air when Clint was knocked on the back of the head.

His vision blacked out before his knees buckled.

TWENTY-NINE

Clint was never fully out. Perhaps he'd taken so many knocks to the head throughout the years that his skull had somehow gotten thicker. Or perhaps some sound had acted as a warning that he could only react to with the quickest of instincts. One shift of his weight or turn of his head could have helped change the blow from a knockout to one hell of a nasty bump. Either way, it didn't feel good.

The sound of blood rushing through his ears faded a bit, only to be replaced by something else. It was a constant grating noise that sounded like rocks sliding over an old washboard. His balance was off as well, making him feel like he was falling even though his legs were stretched out directly in front of him.

Clint opened his eyes, forcing his lids up with a painful almost impossible effort. All he got in return was a real good look at a whole lot of dark shadows on a field of smeared gray. He couldn't seem to draw a deep enough breath to satisfy his lungs. He did, however, realize that the sound he was hearing was actually something being dragged over packed dirt. After trying to move his legs, he found out that he was the something being dragged.

"Put me down!" Clint snapped as he started to twist and kick. He was surprised when his heels stopped being dragged along the ground and his upper body was allowed to drop to the dirt.

Clint's vision was still blurry, which didn't prevent his hand from going to the holster at his hip. This time, he wasn't surprised. The modified Colt wasn't there.

"Where's Mancuso?" asked a voice directly behind Clint.

With every passing second, Clint's eyesight became clearer and the swirling sensation between his ears lessened. Using his hands as well as his feet, Clint scrambled away from the voice he'd just heard while getting his legs beneath him as quickly as possible. It wasn't a graceful way to stand up, but it got the job done. Another surprise came when a strong hand took hold of Clint's elbow and gave him a boost. Once Clint had his balance, he was pushed back a step.

"All right," the voice said. "You're awake. You're on your feet. Now answer my question."

"You the one that bushwhacked me?" Clint asked.

"You were barely knocked off your feet. Don't be such a baby."

"Baby?" Clint snarled while fighting even harder to clear his senses. "Put your gun away and we'll see what kind of a baby I am."

Clint may not have been able to see clearly, but he could definitely make out the shape of a pistol being pointed at him. The man holding that pistol was slightly shorter than Clint and stood like a trap that was about to clamp shut around unsuspecting game. "Just tell me what I want to know," he said, "before your night gets even worse."

"You're asking about Jack Mancuso?"

"That's right. Tell me where he is."

"If I knew that, I'd be there right now."

The other man paused, recoiled slightly, and then leaned toward Clint again to ask, "What were you doing with Selma Coates?"

"We were eating supper," Clint said. "And I was walking her home. What the hell is it to you?" His vision was even clearer now, so Clint turned to look at his surroundings. He'd been dragged into a wide alley that wasn't too far from the street, but far enough to be out of plain sight. "Where is she? What did you do with her?"

"I didn't do anything," the man replied.

"Who the hell are you?"

"That doesn't matter. Who the hell are you?"

Clint laughed and stooped down to prop his hands on his bent knees while he caught his breath. "If you wanted to have a talk, you might have been better off doing it before you cracked me over the head."

"Just tell me. What's your name?"

While Clint was still feeling the pain of getting hit, he'd managed to shake most of the cobwebs out and get his wits about him. He'd played up the act of bending down to catch his breath well enough to get his hands on his knees—and then move.

Clint lunged at him, grabbed the stranger's gun hand, twisted it, and claimed the pistol for himself. Now looking over the top of the pistol's barrel at its surprised owner, Clint noticed something else for the first time. The man was wearing a badge.

"You're only alive because you're a lawman. Now it's up to you to give me a good reason you should stay that way."

THIRTY

"Take it easy, Mister," the man in front of Clint said as he opened his jacket to show more clearly the badge pinned to his shirt underneath. "You're right about me being on the side of the law. So let's just talk like civilized folk."

"Civilized folk don't start their conversations by cracking the other person over the head."

"I know."

"From behind, no less."

The man winced slightly while nodding. His hands were still in front of him and he calmly motioned with them as if to slow down everything in his vicinity. "We got off on the wrong foot. I'll grant you that much. Let's not make it any worse."

Clint studied the man in front of him very carefully before lowering the pistol. "Where's my Colt?" he asked.

Slowly, the other man peeled open his jacket a little further to show the weapon tucked under his belt. "You're welcome to it."

"You're damn right I am. Now toss it."

Narrowing his eyes to watch Clint's gun hand, the man removed the modified Colt from its resting place using only one finger and a thumb. Once it was clear, he snapped his hand forward to send the Colt through the air so Clint could snatch it back.

"How about you return the favor?" the other man asked hopefully.

"Tell me your name first."

"Ben Kaid. How about you?"

Less than a second ticked by before Clint sent the gun he'd taken sailing back to Kaid. By the time that gun was reclaimed, Clint had shifted his Colt to his right hand and hefted it to feel its weight. Satisfied that the pistol was loaded, he replied, "I'm Clint Adams."

Kaid nodded and, looking surprised, said, "I was expecting someone who knew their way around a gun, but not someone like you."

"What's that supposed to mean?"

"It means I would have thought you'd be out of Jack Mancuso's reach."

"You think I'm working for Jack Mancuso?"

"Are you?" Kaid asked.

Letting out a tired sigh, Clint turned his back to the lawman and started walking away. "Fella, I don't have time for this."

"Look, I'm sorry about before. When I saw you with the Coates girl, I thought you were one of Mancuso's men coming to take her away. Did you know those killers are after her so they can get to her father?"

"Yeah, I do know that," Clint said. "Can you tell me where she went?"

Kaid looked around for a few seconds, which was more than enough to tell Clint what he needed to know.

"All right, then," Clint said while resuming his course across the street. "I'll be on my way. Oh," he added while coming to a stop and turning around to face Kaid, "If you so much as think about trying to ambush me again, I won't react as kindly as I did this time around."

With that, Clint holstered his Colt and walked away. Even though the other man was out of his sight, he was preparing for him in every possible way. Clint's ears were open for any footstep that was coming toward him. His hand rested upon the grip of his Colt, ready to draw the weapon at the first hint of trouble.

Kaid didn't make the first attempt to be sneaky as he rushed to catch up with Clint. "We're not through talking yet, Adams!"

"Oh, I think we are."

"How'd you know I was a lawman?"

Since it was clear that he wasn't going to shake loose of the other man so easily, Clint allowed Kaid to fall into step beside him. He decided not to tell the man he'd spotted his badge. "Easy. You didn't shoot me."

Even without looking at Kaid's face, Clint could tell the other man was scowling in either disbelief or confusion. Most likely, it was a bit of both.

"So," Kaid said, "anyone but a lawman would have gunned you down?"

"Instead of talking so much? Yeah. Pretty much."

"That seems a bit farfetched."

"I was right, wasn't I?" Clint pointed out.

Reluctantly, Kaid replied, "Yes, but I think it's more likely that you knew I was coming."

"What difference does it make?"

Clint's progress was stopped by a hand that slapped down firmly onto his shoulder. Although the lawman's grip wasn't enough to halt him in his tracks, Clint wasn't about to be handled by the same man who'd so recently given him a splitting headache.

While there was no mistaking the fire in Clint's eyes, Kaid held firm by maintaining his grip. "The difference," he explained, "is whether or not I've got some element of surprise while dealing with a gang of known killers. Also, if anyone in this town knew I was coming, it means somebody spoke out of turn. In my line of work, that can mean an early grave."

"I've dealt with plenty of lawmen," Clint explained tersely. "I've even worked as one on occasion. You walk like a lawman, talk like a lawman, and fight like a lawman. Let's face it," he added while reaching up to rub the sore spot on the back of his skull, "you wouldn't be the first peace officer to avoid killing someone by using the butt of your pistol instead of its trigger."

"I suppose that makes sense."

"Did you happen to see where Selma Coates went after you knocked me on the back of the head?"

"After I disarmed you," Kaid explained, "she was already gone."

"Well that's a fine bit of marshaling there, Mister Kaid. Why don't you just go back to wherever you came from and let me find her before she winds up getting hurt?"

Clint made it less than a dozen more steps before Kaid spoke up again. Even though they were fairly large steps taken at a swift pace, the lawman never fell very far behind and caught up to him without any trouble.

"Not just marshal," Kaid said in a sterner tone. "I'm a United States Marshal."

"I know. I saw the badge."

"Then you should treat me with a bit more respect."

"Respect is earned," Clint said. "Not given after being bushwhacked."

There weren't many other people around, but Kaid still dropped his voice as if the entire town was listening. "Miss Coates is being threatened and you're a strange man accosting her in the street. It was an honest mistake."

"You're more of a stranger to her than me and as far as accosting her is concerned…"

"I made a mistake. It's over."

Clint stopped and wheeled around so fast that Kaid bumped into him with his next step. The lawman was still bouncing back slightly when Clint gave him a strong shove to put even more space between them. "In case you still haven't noticed, that mistake might have already cost Selma Coates dearly. Until I find her, I'll hold you responsible for her being missing."

"That's bullshit and you know it!"

"Then where is she?"

"It hasn't been that long since we both saw her," Kaid said. "She's got to be close by."

"Or she could be dead."

"She's not dead. Mancuso doesn't work that way."

"That's right," Clint replied. "He doesn't kill them right away. More than likely, he'll put her through some kind of hell doing whatever an animal like him does to a woman to amuse himself for a while before finishing her off. Unless you want to help find her, I suggest you clear a wide path. Trust me when I tell you that you won't get another open shot at the back of my head again."

Clint expected more words from the lawman, but didn't get them. Rather than wait around for Kaid to catch his breath, Clint left him in the dust.

THIRTY-ONE

The first thing Clint did was return to the spot where he'd last seen Selma. It wasn't far away from where Kaid had taken him and according to his pocket watch, it hadn't been very long ago. Right around fifteen minutes by Clint's estimation. Kaid had ambushed him on a street that ran most of the way through town that was covered in plenty of tracks, wagon ruts, and hoof prints. Even so, the freshest tracks to be found still belonged to him and Selma.

As he followed those tracks toward the nearest intersection, Clint prepared himself for another ambush. The best possibility was that he found Selma close by somewhere, frightened and hiding after Kaid's botched bushwhacking. If only her tracks were visible, Clint might have allowed himself to hope for the best. But hers weren't the only tracks and Clint knew better than to blindly hope for the best.

The trail led away from the street, only to end at the boardwalk. There were several shops lined up along that row, as well as a narrow two-floor office marked as belonging to a publisher of books and local newspapers. All of those buildings were dark. Their windows displayed nothing but shadow. Just as Clint was about to move on, he spotted movement deep within one of the stores.

A sign hanging from a rusty hook marked the store as a dress maker specializing in festivities of all kinds. When Clint took a second look through the window, he cursed himself as a fool for being tricked by a simple play of reflected light playing across a frame used to model petticoats. Closer investigation revealed something else behind that large pane of glass. It was something that had more weight to it than a form made of wire. As he continued to stare, Clint swore he could see one of the shadows inside the place shift with a will of its own.

Clint's fingers slipped around the grip of his Colt. The muscles in his right arm tensed for a draw and a quick squeeze of the trigger. His ears even prepared themselves for the familiar bark of a round being discharged followed by the shattering of glass. The movement he'd been waiting for didn't come from the spot where he was looking. Since Clint had been preparing himself for an attack from all sides, he wasn't caught completely off his guard when he heard the squeak of a nearby door being opened.

In one fluid motion, Clint pivoted his body to the right to face the opening door while drawing his Colt and dropping to one knee. His finger tensed around the Colt's trigger, but only enough to cause its hammer to raise slightly from its resting position.

"Jesus Christ," he breathed when he got a look at the frightened face in the dark doorway. "Now's not the time to sneak up on me."

"Sorry," Selma whimpered from where she stood in the entrance to the publisher's building.

Clint lowered the Colt but didn't holster it. "It's all right, Selma," he said. "What the hell happened to you back there?"

"When that man came out of nowhere, I—I just jumped. Jumped back and away." Tears welling in her eyes, she added, "I'm sorry, Clint. I should have stayed to help, but I just...ran."

"There wasn't much you could have done."

But his words barely seemed to register in Selma's ears. "I just ran. I ran and hid like..."

Clint holstered his gun and took her face in his hands so he could look her straight in the eyes. "You did a good thing. You're safe now."

A faint glimpse of a smile drifted across her face. "I thought you were hurt."

"My head's a lot thicker than most," he said. "It'll take a harder knock than that to put me down for long."

"And what about the man who hit you?"

"Don't worry about him. Let's just get you home."

Nodding, Selma stepped out from the doorway. "And what about the other one?" she asked.

Clint had been stepping back to clear a path for her, but stopped to keep her from moving any further from the doorway. "What other one?"

"The other man. The one who came along right after the one who hit you. Didn't you see him?"

"What did he look like?"

Selma was worried again and she no longer attempted to leave the shadows in which she'd been hiding. "About your height, but a little thinner. Black skin."

"Where was he when you saw him last?"

She pointed beyond Clint toward the spot that had caught his eye a scant few moments ago.

"Go home," Clint said

Selma nodded and started to inch her way out through the doorway.

"No," Clint told her. "Run."

THIRTY-TWO

It wasn't Clint's main intention to use Selma as bait. Mostly, he wanted to get her out of the dark, in the open, and on her way back to her house where Derrick Coates could protect her. If she managed to flush out one of the gunmen who'd been hiding nearby, then that would just be a bonus.

Selma emerged from the publisher, took a quick look at Clint, and then bolted like a deer that had been discovered by a pack of dogs. Clint watched the window of the dress maker's shop until he saw something shift within the shadows. It wasn't much of a movement, but it was enough to convince him that something other than tailor's forms were in there.

Instead of waiting around for more signs, Clint positioned himself in front of the entrance, lowered his shoulder, and rammed the front door. The sound of splintering wood filled Clint's ears, washing out just about anything else that he might have heard at that moment. He didn't need to hear the other man hiding within the dress maker's shop, however, to know he was there. Nelson Stamp gave himself away by jumping out from behind the counter where he was hiding and racing for the back of the shop.

"Get back here, you son of a bitch!" Clint snarled while charging through the shop.

133

Nelson's features were dulled by the shadows, but his actions spoke well enough. He darted through the shop without bumping into very many shelves or other obstacles, which was a lot better than Clint. When he heard the metallic click of a pistol's hammer being thumbed back, Clint drew his Colt and fired a quick shot at an upward angle.

Sparks from the Colt's barrel provided enough light to illuminate a blink of time. In contrast to the blackness before and after the shot, that brief glimpse of his surroundings became etched into Clint's mind like the subject of a photograph. He narrowly avoided slamming face first into a tall shelf of folded cloth and steered himself toward an aisle leading to what he thought was a doorway at the back of the place.

Nelson threw open that door and ran through while taking quick aim over his shoulder. Seeing the pistol in the other man's hand, Clint raised his own gun once again to take more careful aim. Pointing the Colt's barrel as if he was pointing his finger at a target, he squeezed the trigger to send a piece of hot lead screaming through the air.

The bullet tore through meat and chipped some bone as it clipped Nelson's gun arm. It might have gotten his hand, but Clint couldn't tell from where he was standing. All he knew for certain was that Nelson wasn't so interested in firing back at him anymore.

While the first shot had given Clint some light with which he could find his way through the store, the second shot damn near blinded him. His eyes suddenly ached from having to adjust to bright flashes of light and near total darkness in such a short amount of time. More than that, a wave of dizziness rolled through him. He could either slow his pace a bit or gamble on not tripping over something or running straight into a wall. Clint picked the former and held his gun in front of him in case another prime target presented itself.

The silhouette of Nelson's body in the rear doorway looked like a smeared charcoal sketch against the dim light coming from outside. Clint ran toward it, but fought the urge to keep running all the way outside. He hadn't lived all these years, through so many gunfights, just to run headlong into such an obvious ambush spot.

First, he kicked the door that was already swinging shut after Nelson had gone through. When that didn't spark any shots from the outside, Clint took a cautious step outside. It may have been dark, but he could see well enough to know empty space when he saw it. The only thing waiting for him on the other side of that door was a small lot that led to a back street and at least two alleys.

Nelson was nearby and he wasn't overly concerned with a fight. Instead, he climbed onto the back of a waiting horse and gripped the saddle horn tightly with his uninjured hand, hoping he'd be able to stay mounted.

"Stop right there!" Clint commanded.

Despite not having as firm a grip as he would have liked, Nelson tapped his heels against the horse's sides to get the animal into a gallop. Less than three steps later, he was struggling to keep from falling out of the saddle and landing on the street.

Clint ran to the horse to try and grab hold of its reins or even snag part of the saddle. Both it and its rider were too spooked to stay still for long and when the horse picked up some speed, Nelson somehow held on.

"Come on," Clint snarled as he sighted along the top of his barrel. "Give me a shot."

Between the muddy swirl within his own senses—his head was still hurting--and the erratic movement of both the horse and its rider, Clint wasn't given much of anything. Since he wasn't about to shoot a horse without a damn good reason, he had to let a few precious seconds tick by. After that, Nelson Stamp was completely out of range.

"Damn it!"

THIRTY-THREE

"How's that feel?" Selma cooed.

Although she was only dabbing at his head with a damp towel, Clint might have sworn she was jabbing at him with an ice pick. He gritted his teeth against the stabbing pain coming from the spot where he'd been hit and did his best to keep from shoving her away amid a storm of obscenities. "It hurts," he said tersely.

"I'll bet it does. It looks terrible."

"Then how about you just leave it alone?"

"I can't do that," she replied while wringing out the towel into a basin on a small table next to the bed. "It needs to be cleaned up, which is exactly what I intend to do."

Clint sat on the edge of a small bed in a room that was decorated in frilly lace and bright colors. It was Selma's room in the Coates house and he wouldn't have been surprised if it was the same one she'd had when she was a little girl. The surroundings had a calming effect on her and, while he wouldn't admit as much out loud, it had the same effect on Clint as well. At least he didn't feel like pummeling someone with his bare hands any longer.

"Take a deep breath," she said in a tranquil tone.

"I'm breathing just fine," Clint snapped while getting to his feet.

"You sound like a bull."

"Bulls are strong and healthy."

"They're also raging animals," Selma pointed out. "And that's what you've been like ever since that man rode away."

"Well let's see how you feel after you get knocked on the head and nearly shot."

"It's over now."

"Is it? Or did you just forget that you're the one that might get kidnapped at any moment?"

Selma's hand suddenly became heavier and came to a rest on Clint's shoulder. When he looked over to her, he found her gazing at the floor with a tight frown on her face. She closed her eyes, blinked a few times, and straightened up again while dipping the towel into the water so she could continue with her task.

"No," she said. "I didn't forget."

Seeing the fear etched deep into her face, Clint suddenly felt like an ass. "Sorry," he said.

"No, you're right. It's not over. I realize that. I just thought it might be over for tonight. At the very least, we could pretend it is so we can get some rest." Her dabbing became faster and her voice more nervous as she hastily added, "Of course, I also know that you need more rest than I do since you've been through..."

Clint took hold of her hand to keep it still. "Just stop. I spoke out of turn. Must be the aching head or perhaps I'm still dizzy."

She smirked uncomfortably and shrugged. "That is a nasty lump on your head. I'm surprised you were only out for less than a minute."

"Actually, I am too. I guess it helps that my head is already full of rocks."

It was good to see a smile crack the frightened visage of Selma's face and Clint immediately wanted to make that smile even brighter.

"Mostly I got lucky," he said.

"How so?"

"The rocks. Weren't you listening?"

She smiled wider and even threw in a little laugh for good measure.

"Nah," Clint sighed. "I was turning at the last moment before the knock landed. Otherwise, it would have knocked me out cold for a good while longer."

"So that man was working with the other one that was following me?" she asked.

"No," Clint said, "He's a US Marshal named Kaid. Ever hear of him?"

Her smile dimmed a bit and she slowly shook her head. "No. Never."

"Ben Kaid?" He gave her the whole name. "Still doesn't sound familiar?"

Selma shook her head again. "No. Sorry."

Clint smiled and made his way back to the bed. Sitting down on its edge, he ran his fingers through his hair in a familiar way, only to hit the sore spot and send a jolt of pain through his body.

"Would you like me to finish cleaning that for you?" she asked.

"I really would."

She picked up the wet towel and climbed onto the bed to kneel behind him. It did them both a lot of good to forget about everything else that was going on for a while and just set their sights on one little problem at a time.

She leaned into him, pressing her breasts against his back, and continued to minister to his sore head.

THIRTY-FOUR

The next morning, Clint walked into the Coates' dining room while steam was still rising from the coffee pot. Derrick Coates seemed somewhat shocked to see a man in such a rumpled state emerge from his daughter's room, but seemed to get over it quick enough. Even so, Clint picked up on the trace of fatherly ire that was stirring within the other man.

"Morning, Adams," Coates said. "I meant to put you in one of the spare bedrooms."

"Your daughter was kind enough to lend me a chair in the corner of hers," Clint replied. Rubbing the top of his head, he added, "I was lucky to make it that far with the dizzy spells I had."

"Oh, that's right! You took a nasty knock, I heard."

"You heard correct, sir."

Whether he was responding to the respect in Clint's tone or the lump on his head, Coates smiled and motioned toward the long dining room table. "Well, have a seat, then. Get some food in your belly and clear the fog from between your ears because we've got some business to discuss."

Clint took the seat he'd been offered and helped himself to some coffee. There were two plates on the table as well, stacked high with griddle cakes and corn bread. "The fog's lifted," he said. "What business did you have in mind?"

Coates took his seat at the head of the table. Although the house was filled with the commotion of a new day getting started, it was only the two of them in the dining room thus far. Pouring himself some coffee and dropping in a lump of sugar, he said, "I've got a proposition for you."

"Another one? That's mighty generous."

"This one would take precedence over the one I offered yesterday. In fact, it would start immediately."

Clint lifted the cup to his mouth and took a sip of the rich, aromatic brew. "I'm listening."

"First of all, I want you to know I ain't helpless or weak."

"I never thought you were, Mister Coates."

"I also ain't stupid. Don't treat me like a fool and we'll get along a whole lot better."

Clint set his cup down and stared the other man directly. "When have I done anything like that?"

"A few moments ago when you told me you slept in a damn chair in my daughter's room."

"I told you that because it's the truth. You're her father and I know it's never easy to think of the attention she might get from men, but she gets it all the same. This is also your house and I have no intention of disrespecting you while I'm in it."

Studying Clint carefully, Coates nodded slowly. It wasn't a signal of agreement, but more of a way for him to digest the words he was hearing. "So you haven't... been with my Selma?"

"That's not what you asked me."

"I'm asking now."

This wasn't the first time Clint had been in a predicament like this one. He'd been held at gunpoint several times as well, but somehow he vastly preferred that to having this conversation with the father of a woman he'd bedded. "If you want to know that sort of thing, I suggest you ask your daughter." Seeing that Coates was about to unleash an angry torrent of words at him then and there, Clint held up one hand to respectfully buy him another second or two.

"To answer your question," Clint said calmly, "Your daughter and I have been together. I imagine you've already pieced together as much already. As for last night in her room, I slept on the chair and she slept in her bed. That's all there was to it."

Coates glared at him for a short while before letting out a tired grunt. One thing about the truth was that it was oftentimes very easy to spot. This being one of those times, Derrick allowed his muscles to relax. "I appreciate you being up front with me, Adams. I'll do the same for you by saying I think any one of us or all of us could wind up dead if we get sloppy."

"I've found that's pretty much always the case."

"The men who threatened me got here a bit sooner than I'd expected and precautions need to be taken. There's no longer enough time for me to use my own resources so I need to use whatever is available to me."

"That sounds like desperation talking," Clint pointed out.

"Not desperation," Derrick said. "Necessity. These men pose a threat right now. Either they know most of my hired hands are out of town for a spell or they just got lucky. Whichever it is, I can't just stand back and let them take what's mine."

"So you want me to stay here and keep an eye on things."

"Just until my men get back."

"How far away are they?" Clint asked.

"No more than a day or two south of San Francisco guarding one of my ships. I've already sent word through San Francisco by telegraph, but it might not reach my foreman's hands until tomorrow."

"If you're lucky," Clint sighed, knowing all too well how many different obstacles could get in the way of any courier. Throw in trouble from outlaws looking to keep that courier silent and the odds became even slimmer.

Judging by the tired expression on Coates' face, he was more than aware of those odds.

"Yeah," he said. "But I haven't gotten where I am through luck alone. Sometimes a man's got to make a tough choice. Sometimes he's got to make a sacrifice. No man worth his salt would choose to sacrifice his kin just to gain a few more dollars in a business transaction."

Clint had crossed paths with quite a few men who would sacrifice a lot more for a lot less. Hearing Coates say those words with such conviction, however, made one of Clint's choices much easier. "All right," he said to the businessman. "I'm guessing you're asking me to stay here and act as an armed guard instead of a scout or escort for some wagons."

"That's correct, Mister Adams. You'll be paid handsomely for your time."

"I'm sure," Clint said, "but money isn't exactly the issue here."

"It isn't?" Coates asked as he looked at Clint with a deeper amount of respect.

"What, exactly, do you expect me to do to earn this handsome compensation?"

"Like you said," Coates answered. "Stay on here and keep watch over my Selma. She told you about the threats made to her in the letter I received, didn't she?"

"She sure did," Clint replied. "What I want to know is how far you expect me to go to earn that pay."

Scowling, Derrick said, "You'll do whatever is necessary, of course."

"Including spilling blood?"

"If you deem that necessary."

"I won't agree to be your assassin," Clint stated plainly. "I wouldn't agree to do that for anyone."

"All right."

"I'll stay to see no harm comes to you or your family, but I'll do it on my terms. I'm not about to become one of your killers."

Suddenly, Coates' features showed a sharp edge. "I don't have killers on my payroll, Mister Adams. And I don't want to see anyone killed. If someone wants to take a shot at my family, however, and won't be stopped by anything other than a bullet through the skull, I'll pull the trigger myself and I'd expect anyone hired to protect Selma to do the same."

"That's what I wanted to hear."

THIRTY-FIVE

There were plenty of men who were content to sit on their laurels and collect any money that might be tossed at them. Those were the sorts of men who took easy jobs or did the least amount of work to get a job done.

There were also plenty of men who took pay for a job while only thinking about where and how they might collect their next chunk of gold. They were greedy dogs not concerned with completing any job at all, but moving on before their misguided employers realized they were gone.

Clint Adams wasn't either of those kinds of men. On the contrary, he looked for ways to get a job done as completely as possible. Every so often, there was a way to get it done quickly without cutting too many corners. In his experience, cutting corners usually resulted in other cuts being made. More often than not, those cuts would be deep, they would hurt, and blood would be drawn.

No matter how well he wanted to do his work, Clint also knew it didn't pay to be in too much of a hurry. It wasn't a sense of rushing the task at hand that lit a fire under Clint after he accepted Derrick Coates's proposal. There was something else that gnawed at him like a tick that had dug deep into his guts and wouldn't leave him be.

There was more going on that was just out of his reach. Clint knew it was there, like an unseen predator rustling through the brush away from a camp. He didn't need to have the threat exposed in firelight to know it was stalking him. In fact, any man who relied only on what he saw would find himself being torn apart by that predator before the rays of another dawn found him.

Something was circling Ola Blanca.

Obviously, Jack Mancuso and his men were part of it, but Clint was certain they weren't the whole thing.

"Damn it," he snarled under his breath. Even as he thought about that, he knew that wasn't exactly what bothered him either. There was more. If Mancuso and his men were the only other killers, then there was something else Clint was missing. There was something important that would make all the difference and for the moment, it was still out of his reach.

Like any other stalking predator, this unseen something couldn't be left to its own devices. It needed to be hunted before it sank its fangs into another victim. Clint may not have known where every piece of the puzzle was, but he had a good idea of where to look for the next one.

THIRTY-SIX

Clint knocked on the door of Granny's Boarding House on Main Street. He was immediately greeted by a friendly looking man with wisps of gray hair sprouting from his scalp and a patch of silver stubble on his chin. "Howdy," the man said. "Need a room?"

"Actually," Clint said, "I'd like to talk to Margie."

Smile still intact, the old man replied, "She's out shopping for supper fixins. I can set you up with whatever you need."

"I'd prefer to talk to her. It's not about a room."

"Mind if I ask what it is about, then?"

Even though he never found himself in a spot where he needed to pay for such a service, Clint said, "I'm looking for some companionship. I was told I could look here for it."

The old man looked Clint up and down, deciding eventually that he liked what he saw because the door swung open instead of the other way. "Come on in," he said. "But I can still help you."

Once he was inside, Clint said, "I'd still like to talk to Margie."

"Why? Her ass or anything else on her is for sale, if that's what yer after."

"It's nothing like that." Scowling a bit, Clint added, "I take it you're not her husband."

"Me? Her husband? Hell no! I have worked for the old cow for over fourteen years, which might make us married in some parts of the country." By now, he'd made his way into the next room, waddling like a wooden penguin. "What's on yer mind, Mister?"

Clint followed him into the next room, which was the same one in which he'd eaten not too long ago. All of the chairs were set upside down on top of the tables and there was no sign of life coming from the kitchen. The old timer pulled one chair down, set it upright, and then plopped down onto it with a beleaguered sigh.

"So," the old man said, "if you don't need a room for the night and you ain't in the market for pussy, what brings you here?"

"I was told that Margie knows about all the girls working in this town."

"You mean the whores?" the old man asked. In his voice, there was no insult or an attempt to jostle Clint's sensibilities. He was just stringing his words together in the most natural way.

"Yeah," Clint replied.

Making a fist with one hand, the old man popped out his thumb and then hooked it back toward his chest. "Then you can talk to me. Name's Billy."

Clint took down another chair, spun it around, and sat on it with his chest against the backrest. "It's not for me. Actually, from what I heard, Margie handles most of the appointments for the town's girls."

"You make it sound like a damn industry. There's four, sometimes five girls spreading their knees apart for pay in Ola Blanca. Depends on whether their womanly tides are in or out, know what I mean?"

"Yes."

"The monthly bleedin'," Billy said. "That's what—"

"Yeah. I understood the first time."

Billy leaned to one side so he could prop an elbow on the table closest to him. With the other hand, he opened and closed his fist to work the kinks from his gnarled joints. "I understand, too. Y'see, the business of runnin' whores ain't that complicated. So if you don't think you can deal with me, you must either think I'm stupid or you got some kind of deal with Margie on the side. Let me tell you somethin', Mister," Billy added as he pointed a small pistol at Clint's heart. "I don't much like either of them things."

THIRTY-SEVEN

Clint had barely seen the old man move his hand. The fact that there was now a gun in that same hand was even more of a surprise. Even so, he knew he could easily pull his Colt and put Billy down if he so desired. For the time being, that wasn't what he wanted. But the way this talk was progressing, Clint guessed that opinion could change very quickly.

"Hold on now," Clint said in the calmest voice he could manage under the circumstances. "You can just put that gun away right now."

"Oh can I? Are you gonna tell me what to do in my own place?"

Clint still wasn't about to panic. "Look," he said calmly, "you're getting all riled up over nothing."

"Nothing?" Billy's scowl turned into an angry glare, but Clint remained calm. When Billy raised his pistol and tightened his finger around its trigger, Clint got a bit more concerned.

"Nothing!" Billy roared. "That bitch sent you, didn't she?"

"What the hell is wrong with you?" Clint asked as he got to his feet and took a cautious step back.

"Don't put on an act for me. I ain't stupid! That bitch sent you to put a bullet into me!"

"Who?"

"Margie! That's who." Shaking his head, Billy moved his lips to form words that Clint couldn't hear. The faraway look in the old man's glazed eyes suggested those words weren't meant for Clint or anyone else apart from whatever demons infected his addled brain.

The only thing keeping Billy alive this long was the desire in Clint's heart to do everything he could to avoid shooting a crazy old coot. He kept backing up until he bumped against another table. "I haven't lifted a finger to hurt you, Billy," Clint said. "All I've been doing is asking questions here."

"And them questions don't mean shit. You just wanted to git me in here alone so you could kill me!"

Clint shook his head. "I would have been just fine talking to you outside. You're the one that—"

"I heard enough outta you!" Billy said as he narrowed his eyes into a purposeful stare and sighted along the top of his gun's barrel.

Even before the other man's words were out of his mouth, Clint knew Billy was going to shoot. It was a tension that crackled through the air like static just before a thunderstorm really cut loose. That left Clint with two options: shoot first or get out of the way. For the moment, at least, it was an easy choice to make and Clint reached back to grab one of the chairs off the table behind him so he could throw it at Billy.

The older man took his shot, but his aim was thrown way off when he tried to avoid getting hit by the incoming piece of furniture. The bullet punched into a wall somewhere. Clint didn't know any more than that because he was busy sliding over the top of the table while shoving away the rest of the chairs. The weight of his body caused the table to tilt as he reached the far edge, bringing the whole thing down as he hit the floor.

For the most part, that had been Clint's plan. Once he was on the floor, the table acted as a makeshift barricade between him and the old gunman. "I don't know what the hell is troubling you, Billy," Clint called out, "but it's got nothing to do with me!"

"The hell you say!" Billy replied as he fired two quick shots. The first one chipped off a piece of the table's edge and the second knocked a hole clean through.

That second shot was about a foot away from hitting him, but Clint wasn't about to sit still long enough for Billy to improve his aim. Holding his Colt in hand, Clint shouted, "I'll tell you this one more time, old man. I'm not in league with Margie and for that matter, I don't even know why she'd want to be in league with anyone else. I just had some questions, is all."

"You! You'd best have a damn good explanation for all'a this!"

"That's what I'm trying to tell you," Clint said, doing his best to keep calm. "If you'd just give me a second."

"I found your goddamn assassin," Billy roared. "And don't look at me like that!"

Clint still had his back against the overturned table, which meant he couldn't see Billy. Wondering what the old man was talking about, he chanced a glimpse around his cover to find Billy starring at something in the next room. Clint was still turning to see what it was when a shotgun blast filled the room with deafening thunder.

"Shit!" Clint said as he dropped down again.

Billy fired a shot that was immediately answered by the shotgun's second barrel. After that, the only thing Clint could hear was a ringing in his ears.

THIRTY-EIGHT

oping the shotgunner didn't already have another weapon in his hand, Clint rolled away from the table he'd been using for cover and popped up to one knee. His eyes and his Colt both tracked in the same direction as the rest of his body prepared for a fight.

"Oh," Margie said as she fed two fresh shells into the shotgun she carried. "It's you. What's your name again?"

"Clint Adams."

"Right." The old woman closed her shotgun and then cradled it in her arms like a skinny grandbaby. "What were the questions you wanted to ask me?"

Still kneeling with his pistol at the ready, Clint replied, "The first one that comes to mind is what the hell all this shooting was about?"

She stood in the doorway connecting the dining room to the smaller area used as the boarding house's front lobby. Shrugging, she said, "I came in through the side door when I heard the two of you having your little talk. Billy has been getting skittish lately, which is why I was sneaking inside in the first place. Once I saw him swinging his gun around, I thought I should step in."

Clint turned to look at the other side of the room. Billy was sprawled over the chair that had been thrown at him and wasn't moving a muscle. From where Clint was, he could only see the old man's legs, and one arm with the rest of Billy resting on the floor behind the chair. Judging by the chunks that had been ripped from the table and other chairs by the shotgun, as well as the blood splattered over those tables and chairs, Billy wasn't going to move anytime soon.

Climbing to his feet, Clint holstered his Colt and faced Margie. "Normally I don't like to pry," he said. "But I think I've earned more of an explanation than that."

"You sure have," she told him. "How about I give it to you over a stiff drink somewhere away from this mess?"

"Now that sounds like a good idea."

After propping the shotgun in a corner behind a coat rack, Margie led Clint out of the boarding house and to a saloon across the street. Not only did everyone outside and in the saloon seem oblivious to the shots that had been fired nearby, but every face they encountered bore a beaming smile intended for the old woman. She returned the smiles with grunts and lazy waves while making her way straight to the bar inside the saloon.

"The usual," she said to the barkeep.

The man behind the bar nodded and took a bottle from its spot on the shelf.

Pointing to the bottle, Margie added, "Just hand that over, along with two glasses."

"Sure thing, Margie," the bartender said.

The old woman went to a table at the back of the room, cradling her bottle in a similar fashion that she'd cradled the shotgun earlier. Clint followed and sat down across from her when she lowered herself onto a creaky chair.

"Billy's my business partner," she said as she poured some whiskey from the bottle into both glasses. "Or he was, if he's dead."

"Oh, I'd say it's a good bet that he's dead," Clint replied.

"Good. That old fool's been threatening to kill me for a few weeks now."

"Why?"

Margie took a drink of her whiskey before replying, "He thought I was swindling money from his share of the whores we run in this town as well as the next one over."

"Were you?" Clint asked.

"Course I was! Billy may have been a fool, but he weren't stupid."

Rather than ask how that statement was supposed to make any sense, Clint took a drink of whiskey as well. He generally wasn't fond of that kind of liquor, but it did help get him through the conversation he was having.

"I intended on sending some young men over to knock some sense into him," Margie continued. "Or at least knock him around hard enough for him to leave town like I asked him to."

"And I take it he wanted to stay."

"Yep. I always thought it'd be good if I could just kill him and be done with it." She raised her glass to Clint. "Thanks to you, I got a real good excuse to do just that."

"It doesn't seem like people around here are too concerned about folks shooting each other. Either that," Clint said, "or they're all deaf."

"This is a rough part of town. Also, these folks know about the problems me and Billy were having. I'd imagine most of 'em are just glad it's over and I'm the one to walk out of here. When I run things, my girls are a lot happier. And when my girls are happy, most of the men in town are happy. Just to be sure, though..."

Margie pushed back from the table, lifted her glass over her head, and announced, "Pussy will be half price all week!"

That was greeted by a rousing chorus of shouts from the rest of the saloon.

"Starting tomorrow!" she quickly added. "Momma's gotta clean her house first."

Some more members of the crowd shouted back at her and none of them had a single nice thing to say about Billy.

"I guess that means you won't have to worry about anyone calling the law regarding the shooting," Clint said.

"The law?" she chuckled. "You mean him?"

Clint turned to where she was looking, expecting to see a familiar face. Instead of the lawman he'd already met in town, he saw a pudgy man with a bulbous red nose leaning against the bar wearing a crooked grin. He also wore a badge pinned to a sweat stained shirt.

"No," Clint replied. "Not him."

"He's the only law in town."

"I don't think so."

The good natured woman who'd just made every man in that saloon so happy was nowhere to be found when Margie leaned across the table to scowl at Clint. "Are you another fucking lawman?" she asked.

"No," Clint replied, and more than a little happy to give that response. "I crossed paths with a US Marshal by the name of Ben Kaid. Ever hear of him?"

The sour expression remained etched deeply into Margie's features. The majority of her ire was no longer aimed at Clint, however, when she said, "That prick's been through town once or twice. He always knew better than to stay for long, though."

"I can't see why. This is such a welcoming place."

For a second, it seemed that the old lady was just as likely to slap Clint's face as she might rub his shoulder. Instead, when she held her hand a few inches over the table, she dropped it straight down again hard enough to get everything on it quaking.

"I like men with a sense of humor!" she said. "And handsome ones are even better. Drink up, Adams! We got some celebrating to do!"

THIRTY-NINE

Clint may not have been in a mood to celebrate, but he wasn't about to deny Margie the pleasure. He was even happier to watch her drain that bottle of whiskey she'd purchased for the occasion. For every gulp of whiskey Clint took, she downed five. While the old girl held her liquor better than most men Clint knew, she became much more talkative as the night wore on.

"Adams," she said in a slight slur, "you don't even know how much I owe you for what you did. Billy was a dirty piece of...of...dirt!"

"Those are the worst kind," he said in a voice that he textured with a bit of added drunkenness. Clint was no stage actor, but he did a good enough job to convince his bleary-eyed audience of one.

"They sure are!" she said merrily while refilling Clint's glass. "Now what the hell were you doing over at my boarding house anyway? You don't strike me as the sort of man who'd pay for pussy."

"You are very observant, Margie."

"I been called worse."

"I'm looking for some men who probably just got into town," Clint said.

She looked at him silently for a moment before saying, "You also don't strike me as the sort of man looking to be with other men."

"I was coming to you because I figured these men would be known to some of your girls," he said to clear the air. "It's been my experience that the people in any town who know who comes and goes are the barkeeps and the madams. Since you handle a good amount of business in Ola Blanca..."

"You thought you'd come straight to Grandma Margie," she said through a beaming smile. "Smart man."

"I also figured a woman in your line of work would want to keep on the right side of the lawmen around here."

Suddenly, Margie didn't seem so drunk. Looking at Clint through sharp eyes and a guarded expression, she said, "There's a bit more to you than I thought, Adams."

"Likewise."

"Why were you poking around my place?"

"I had some questions to ask you," Clint replied.

"You could've asked Billy. He likes to act like the big dog."

"But he wasn't the one in charge. You are. That wasn't too hard to see."

"Not for you, maybe. Is this about that US Marshal?"

"Partly. What do you know about him?"

Margie's face twisted up as if her last sip of whiskey had gone sour. "He only comes around when he wants something, throwing his weight around and being a pain in the ass. Just like every other lawman."

"What did he want this time?" Clint asked.

"He was asking about kidnappers and outlaws. I told him I didn't know of any."

Now, Clint's eyes narrowed and he leaned forward as if he was sharing a secret with a trusted friend. "But that wasn't true, now was it?"

Margie smiled, not as a willing confidante, but as someone who no longer had to go through the motions of lying about what was going through her mind. "Now what kind of hostess would I be if I let the law barge in on my guests when they're in the middle of having their fun?"

"I'm not the law."

"And that's why I'm still talking to you."

Perhaps Margie's guard wasn't completely lowered by the whiskey as Clint had hoped, but she was obviously more relaxed after having her drinks. It was very possible that she was thinking the same of him, which only greased the wheels even further.

"Who were the men that US Marshal was after?" he asked.

"Jack Mancuso and a few of his boys," she replied without hesitation.

"Do you know where they are?"

"One of them stopped by, but he wasn't staying in town for long."

"Are you sure about that?"

She nodded and leaned back into her seat. "They've come through before and every time, they pay for some time with at least one of my girls."

"They've all come through here?"

"That's right. Don't ask me about their business here because that's none of my concern. In case you're wondering, I didn't tell that lawman anything about Mancuso or his boys."

"Why not?"

When she lifted her glass, she reached out to bump it against the one still in Clint's hand. "Because most lawmen are worse than an ignorant cowboy looking to get with one of my girls. They want what they want and they

165

want it right away. Don't give a damn about patience, manners, or anything else apart from their own desires. Even though I make my living off of that sort of thing, it's not anything I'd tolerate without getting paid."

Clint understood all too well. When things got rough, it was all too easy to get wrapped up in the storm until a man became another storm all unto himself. There was no underestimating the value of taking some time to share a few drinks and some laughs.

"Are any of them still in town?" he asked.

"If they are," Margie replied, "they're laying real low. You ask me, they aren't the sorts of fellows who lie low for long. I'd say they moved on."

"I saw one of them not too long ago."

"You mean Nelson?"

"That's the one," Clint replied.

"Whatever he was after, he's got it already," Margie said with absolute confidence.

"You certain?"

"Mancuso and all of them boys who ride with him can't cross the street without making a commotion. Trust me, when men like that sneak around on their own, it ain't for long. Besides, it doesn't sound to me like they were even doing much in the way of sneaking."

"What makes you say that?"

Margie took a drink of her whiskey and swirled the rest in her glass. "Because you saw him. An outlaw that can't do a bit of sneaking without being seen doesn't stay alive for long and when he gets caught, he bites and claws worse than a cornered rat."

"Yeah," Clint said under his breath as he went through his last meeting with Nelson in his head.

"Obviously, you didn't catch him," she continued. "Because you would've mentioned him being shot or dead."

"I did spot him sneaking around and he bolted. Had a horse waiting for him."

Her eyebrows went up and she shrugged her shoulders. "I could always be wrong. Maybe he just skinned out because he was scared. Speaking of skinning out, if you see that Marshal, do me a favor and point him in another direction until I get Billy dumped somewhere."

That's when the pieces fell into place like a picture that finally came to focus within Clint's mind. He balled up a fist and grunted, "I'll be damned."

FORTY

lint was almost back at the Coates home when he spotted Selma. She was hurrying around the house, heading for the stables where the family's horses and Eclipse were being kept. When she saw him, her eyes became wide enough for him to see from a distance.

"Clint! There you are!"

"Where's your father?" he asked.

"Gone."

"Gone where?" When he didn't get a response to that, Clint hurried forward to take hold of Selma. Gripping her arms tightly, he asked, "Where did he go?"

"He went to have a word with some lawman."

"Local law or a US Marshal?"

She blinked her eyes quickly, flustered by Clint's manner and the grip he refused to relinquish. Twisting her arms from his hands, she said, "It wasn't the town law. Go and see him if you want."

"Where are they?"

"Whenever my father meets with someone, it's at the Joline Steakhouse on Third."

Being familiar enough with the town after his short stay to picture where that was, Clint nodded and turned to face that direction. Before heading off, he asked, "What were you doing out here?"

"Aren't I allowed to leave my home? What's wrong with you, Clint?"

"There are men after you," he said. "Use your head."

"I can take care of myself," she said defiantly.

Taking half a step toward her, Clint snapped, "Now it's my job to take care of you, so do as I say and get inside. Please, just stay in the house until I can be certain that it's safe."

"You're scaring me, Clint. What happened?"

"I just thought of something that could make a big difference in what's happening between your father and the men who've been threatening him. I'll talk to him and when I come back I'll let you know the rest. For now, though, please…"

She spun away from him while holding her hands up. "I know, I know. You want me to hide in the house like a frightened little cat."

"It's not that."

"I'll do what you asked," she said in a softer tone of voice. "But I want to hear everything you two talked about when you get back."

"You'll be the first to know," Clint assured her. "After all, it concerns you the most."

"All right, then. Joline's is on the corner. It's a little place with a balcony on the second floor. Daddy's table is all the way in the back. Even if the place is closed, just go right in. He'll be there."

Clint ran all the way to Joline's, knowing he didn't have much time to speak to Derrick Coates. When he got there, he found a small restaurant with only a slight glow of light coming from behind drawn curtains. Following Selma's instructions to the letter, he shoved open the front door and went all the way to the back of the dining room where a single table was lit by a lantern hanging on the wall behind it.

Someone inside the place shouted for Clint to stop or say who he was. Clint ignored them and went to Derrick Coates instead. By the time he got there, he was staring down the barrel of a gun that had been drawn by the man sitting beside him.

"Adams?" Marshal Kaid said from behind the pistol in his hand. "What's the meaning of this?"

"I'd like to know that myself," Derrick added.

"Those thieves aren't after your daughter," Clint announced, not at all concerned with the gun being pointed at him. Even as rough hands took hold of his from behind, he kept his attention focused on the men at the table. "They're after something else. I'd guess it's the shipment."

"Which shipment?" Derrick asked.

Pulling free of the man who'd grabbed him, Clint turned to get a look at a big fellow who'd probably been charged with guarding Joline's front door. "The shipment that's not being accompanied by any armed men now that you've sent for your guards to come here!"

Kaid slapped his hand against the table. "I told you there was going to be trouble with a shipment and you told me there wasn't any sort of problem with anything!"

"There isn't," Derrick insisted.

"Then what the hell is all this about?" Kaid asked while waving his free hand at Clint.

"This," Derrick sighed, "is precisely the reason why I didn't want to make any of this known."

"Too late for that," Clint said. "What were the two of you meeting about anyway in the middle of the night?"

It wasn't until that moment that Kaid remembered he had his gun drawn. Holstering the pistol, he said, "I had it on good authority that someone in Mister Coates's company sold him out to some outlaws looking to rob one of his shipments. Maybe even the same ones that have been kidnapping rich men's family members to use as leverage against them."

Derrick put his face in his hands as though he wanted to hide himself from the world around him. "I wasn't supposed to get anyone involved," he groaned through his fingers. "Now it's all gone to hell."

"It went to hell a while ago," Clint said. "Everything that's happened over the last few days has just been a ruse."

"What now?" Kaid asked, looking every bit as confused as Coates.

"Something bothered me this whole time, but I couldn't quite put my finger on it," Clint explained. "Starting with why you'd get a letter announcing the kidnappers' intentions before they had what they were after."

"It was a threat," Derrick said.

"But it didn't do any good," Clint replied. "Unless it was only meant to get you riled up. Then you were riled up even further until you called in your best hired guns to protect your daughter."

"Leaving that shipment open," Kaid said. "Damn!"

"How'd they know which shipment would be guarded?" Derrick asked. "Or that there even was a shipment worth stealing on its way out for delivery?"

"Because there's someone on the inside feeding them information," Kaid snapped. "That's what I've been trying to tell you, Derrick! NOW will you listen to me for Christ's sake?"

But Derrick kept shaking his head in a daze. "I don't give that many people such information. And the men I got working for me who do know all have proven themselves to me more times than I can count. Hell, most of them stand to lose more by having that shipment stolen than they could gain. It just doesn't make sense!"

"What if it wasn't a man that double crossed you?" Clint asked.

"What are you saying?"

Before Clint could explain himself any further, someone charged through the front door, still ajar after Clint had made his entrance. This time, the fellow who'd grabbed hold of Clint was quick to storm the uninvited guest.

"Mister Coates!" the breathless new arrival said. "Your…"

In the next instant, the man acting as guard in the restaurant plowed straight into the other man with his shoulder. It wasn't until then that Clint saw the deputy's badge pinned to the first man's shirt. The deputy, who was the same man that had grabbed Clint earlier, held on to the fellow who'd most recently stormed Joline's like he was displaying a fish dangling from a hook.

"Your stables!" the breathless fish said. "Mister Coates! Your stables!"

Derrick jumped to his feet. "What about my stables, Will?"

Now struggling to wriggle free of the deputy, Will sputtered incoherently as his feet slapped against the floor.

"Let him go!" Kaid demanded.

The deputy did as he was told, allowing Will to slip from his grasp.

"Your stables," Will said in a rush. "They're on fire!"

FORTY-ONE

lint, Coates, the marshal and his deputy all ran straight to the Coates place. Well before they arrived, they could see the glow of flames reaching up into the sky. Along the way, one of their fears was put to rest when they heard the rumble of hooves beating against the ground. A couple of horses could be seen racing in another direction, but one in particular headed straight for the group of men racing down the street.

"There you are, boy," Clint said as he reached out to take Eclipse's nose in his hands. "Great to see you!"

They made their way back to the stables, gathering up neighbors who'd stuck their heads out of their homes to see what was going on. Once they arrived at the stables, something other than the sight of the large pyre made their stomachs clench.

"You smell that?" Clint asked.

"Yeah," Coates said. "Kerosene."

"There won't be much we can do about that fire," Kaid said, "apart from watch it burn."

While none of the other men admitted as much out loud, the US Marshal was right. Flames tore through the wooden structure like an unholy storm, fueled by the kerosene that stuck to the back of Clint's throat. Although several locals came to help with the effort of dousing the fire, it was too late to save the stables. Between the dry wood, the straw, and the kerosene, the entire building collapsed in hardly any time at all.

Clint rolled up his sleeves and joined the bucket brigade that was busy containing the blaze. Thanks to the efforts of him and Derrick's neighbors, the fire didn't spread to any of the other nearby structures. One man was missing from the brigade. He was the same man that called out in a voice that was equal parts desperation and fear.

"Selma!" Coates hollered. "Selma, baby, where are you?"

Nobody answered him.

"Selma!" Coates shouted as he rushed into the smoldering pile of rubble that had once been his stables. He was kept from getting too far into the burning wreckage when his friends and neighbors took hold of him, but he struggled to break free so he could sift through it with his bare hands.

Because the stables were relatively isolated from any other buildings, the fire ended almost as quickly as it had begun. Neighbors expressed their concerns to some of the familiar faces Clint recognized from the times he'd been inside the Coates home, but Coates wouldn't remove himself from the spot where his stables had been. Once the flames were extinguished and only thick ash and smoke remained, he waded through the broken lumber shouting his daughter's name.

Clint stood by and watched, knowing all too well that there was nothing he could do to alleviate the other man's troubled mind.

Marshal Kaid stood beside him, sweating from the heat and hard work he'd contributed to the efforts to put the fire out. "That girl may not even be in town for all we know," he said. "I haven't seen her."

"I have," Clint replied.

"You think she had something to do with setting this blaze?"

"We could ask her if we could find her."

Looking around at the people standing near the smoking pile of rubble, Kaid asked, "You think she's in the house?"

"If she is," Clint said, "I'll eat my hat."

FORTY-TWO

The fire had been raging behind her when Selma tore out of Ola Blanca on the back of her favorite horse. Her lips had been curved into a smile and her chest heaved with excited breaths as she'd snapped her reins to get the animal beneath her to move faster. It was a straight path to the row of three trees situated near a small pond that had been the spot where she'd always told boys to meet her when she'd been growing up. It had been the spot where she'd lost her virginity and taken the innocence of many young men afterward.

On the night the stables burned to the ground, Selma Coates met up with two men. It wasn't the first time for that either, but these two men weren't there waiting to get their hands under her skirts. They waited for her arrival with stony expressions and grim intent swirling in their eyes.

Barely reining her horse to a stop, Selma jumped down from the saddle and approached the pair of men waiting there. "I did it," she said proudly. "Just like you told me."

"You set the fire?" Jack Mancuso asked.

"Yes."

"With the kerosene?" Nelson wanted to know. "That's important. Otherwise, it won't burn fast enough to get the job done."

"I used all the kerosene we had," she replied. "It went up like a tinderbox as soon as I lit the fire. All the horses bolted to cover my tracks but I waited until I was well away from my house before riding at a full gallop."

"Was anyone following you?" Mancuso asked.

"Do I look like an idiot?" she scoffed.

"Answer the goddamn question."

When she looked over to Nelson, Selma received a curt nod. She let out a labored breath while bringing her gaze back to Mancuso as if she was raking her eyeballs over a field of hot coals. "Nobody followed me," she told him. "Trust me. I've made this ride dozens of times."

"And you're certain your pappy did what he was supposed to do?" Mancuso asked.

Selma worked her way closer to Nelson's side. When she reached up to touch his leg, her hair was grabbed so he could roughly force her to look straight at him. "Answer him," Nelson told her. "It's important."

"Yes," she said while gazing up at Nelson. "He got scared enough to send word to the men guarding his shipment for them to come here and help guard me instead."

"When did he send word?"

"Yesterday."

"So that gives us a few days at least," Mancuso said. "Even if they find out what's happening, they won't have enough time to get any men back to where they're supposed to be to guard all them valuables. Any chance them wagons could've been sent somewhere else?"

Selma shook her head while reaching up to stroke the hand that gripped her hair. "The man who is getting the delivery needs it on time. All of Daddy's customers have to stick to their schedule. Besides, there's only one trail to choose from that'll get them where they need to go anywhere close to when they're supposed to be there."

Letting go of his grip on her, Nelson asked, "What's in that shipment again?"

"Antiques," Selma replied. "Some of it's gold and some has some jewels embedded in them, but the pieces are worth a lot more than just the gold and emeralds."

"Damn well better be," Nelson snarled.

Selma's body trembled as if his roughly spoken words had been a hot whisper in her ear.

"I ain't worried about any of that," Mancuso said. "The biggest jobs I've ever pulled off were stealing pieces of art or some other kind of old, fancy trinkets. Rich men pay through the nose for that kind of shit and they don't much care who they deal with just so long as they leave with them trinkets in hand. In fact, they get a bit of a thrill dealing with men like us instead of the usual dealers. Gives 'em a sense of being bad men themselves. Long as their money spends, I don't give a rat's ass."

Nelson looked down at Selma, stroking her hair as he said, "They ain't the only ones who like bad men."

"We ain't got time for this bullshit," Mancuso grunted. "Terrance is meeting us a few miles from here and I don't want to leave him alone for very long. He's been getting twitchy ever since we decided to play this job differently than the others." Glaring directly at Selma, he asked, "You sure this is gonna be worth it?"

"I know my daddy better than anyone," she said. "Taking this shipment will be a simple matter of showing up at the right place at the right time."

"It better be. Otherwise, that pretty little ass of yours will be buried beneath a shallow mound of dirt someplace nobody will ever find."

FORTY-THREE

Mancuso, Nelson, and Selma rode a short way that night and set out early the following day. By the time night fell again, they were outside of San Francisco and heading south. It was early evening on the third day of their ride that they caught sight of two wagons being pulled by two horses each.

The robbery went off without a hitch. With no men to guard the wagons coming from the ship, all the outlaws needed to do was storm the little caravan and show their guns. One of the drivers showed some backbone by firing his shotgun at Nelson. He caught a bullet through the back of the head that was fired by the man who'd been following the wagons for some time.

"Looks like we'll need a new driver," Terrance said as he rode up to the wagons.

Mancuso drank in the sight of the man driving the second wagon. Terror rolled off of him like smoke and might very well have choked him to death if a round from Mancuso's pistol didn't kill him a second later. "Make that two drivers," he said while searching the area surrounding the trail. "Let's get these wagons turned around before anyone comes along to stand in our way."

"There won't be anyone else," Selma insisted. "I told you that a hundred times already."

"Tell your bitch to shut her mouth," Mancuso snarled to Nelson.

Although Nelson didn't follow the order to the letter, he motioned for her to keep quiet and Selma obliged.

"Why are we turning these wagons around?" Terrance asked as he climbed into one of the driver's seats and shoved the freshly made corpse over the side.

"Because we're headed back into San Francisco, that's why," Mancuso said.

"I thought we just left that place."

"We did. That's also the place where we're meeting the man who's buying this load from us."

"Shouldn't we keep it for a while to see if we can get a better price?"

"Do you even know what the hell that stuff is?" Mancuso asked while jabbing a finger at the wagons.

Since he was closest to the side of his wagon, Nelson took a gander through the side window. All he saw was a few short stacks of crates held down with rope and leather straps. "Not exactly, but it's gotta be valuable. Surely we can just sell it for however much the gold and such is worth."

"The gold and such are worth ten thousand," Mancuso said. "Maybe twenty if we can find someone who wants the whole mess. My man in San Francisco is willing to pay fifty for the lot, just so long as the merchandise is in good condition."

Nelson and Terrance looked at each other, shrugged, and settled in with reins in their hands. "Whatever you say, Jack," Terrance declared.

FORTY-FOUR

The hotel room wasn't the fanciest in San Francisco, but it was close. The carpeting was dark red and almost deep enough to hide a man's feet as he made his way to the large, four-post bed. Nelson Stamp wasn't as concerned with the bed or the silk sheets covering it as he was with the woman laying on her stomach in the middle of it.

Selma Coates faced the other direction, gazing out the window, resting her chin upon one hand while idly kicking her feet back and forth. Her breasts pressed against the silk sheets as her naked skin rubbed against the extravagant material. Every time her feet kicked through the air, her round buttocks shook ever so slightly.

"We're gonna be rich," she said idly.

Nelson came up behind her, stripping off his clothes and freeing his hard cock. "Yeah," he said while reaching out to massage her hips. "We are."

"And I won't have to beg my family for money anymore. I can do whatever I want. Go wherever I want and I don't have to wait for Daddy to die before getting what's rightfully mine."

"Your father tried to hold you back?"

"Yes. Every day of my life."

"Best thing for that is to do whatever strikes your fancy."

185

Selma stretched out to grip the other side of the mattress while arching her back. Shifting her legs so her ass rose up and she was on her knees, she looked back with her face pressed against the silk sheets and said, "So what are you waiting for?"

Still holding her by the hips, Nelson pulled her close while easing his rigid penis between her thighs. The tip of his erection found the wet lips of her pussy and with a gentle push, he was inside of her. Selma let out a throaty moan and closed her eyes, savoring every second as he filled her with his thick pole.

At first, Nelson moved slowly in and out of her. He leaned back and buried his cock in her as far as it would go, feeling her moist, warm body fully envelop him. He rubbed the sides of her body before leaning forward to cup her breasts while pumping into her from behind.

Selma moaned softly at first. Her voice rolled around in the back of her throat as her head lolled back and forth. When she felt him thrust a little deeper, she whipped her hair straight back and gripped the bed even tighter. Nelson drove into her with stronger thrusts and then smacked the side of her ass with one open hand.

"That's it," Selma said. "Give it to me. Give it all to me!"

Placing one hand at the small of her back, Nelson grabbed a fistful of her hair with the other hand. He fucked her with a steady rhythm for a few more seconds before pulling back on her hair and burying his cock into her as deep as it could go. The sound she made then wasn't anywhere close to speech. It was more of an animalistic grunt as she spread her legs wider and hung her head low.

Nelson bared his teeth as sweat broke out on his brow. Every muscle in his body worked to drive his stiff cock in and out of her as his pleasure grew to its peak. He could feel her lips tightening around him, so Nelson reached between her legs to rub the sensitive nub of her clit. All he needed to do from there was pump into her a few more times to turn Selma's entire body into a quivering mass.

"God," she wheezed. "God DAMN!"

She clawed at the bed as her climax rolled through her from head to toe. Just when it seemed she was through, Nelson eased partway out of her and pounded into her one last time. Selma's head snapped up and her mouth hung open, unable to push a single sound out.

Eventually, her eyes closed lazily and a tired smile crept onto her face. She crawled forward just enough for him to slip out of her and then turned around to face him. "What do you want, baby?" she asked.

"You know what I want."

She smiled wider, crawled over the top of the bed, and climbed down to the floor. Going straight to her knees, Selma ran her hands along Nelson's legs before reaching up to cup him with both hands. "This what you want?" she purred.

"Yeah," Nelson replied. When he felt her lips wrap around his cock, he put his hands on top of her head and closed his eyes.

Selma sucked the tip of his cock while using her tongue on him. She rubbed him with both hands and teased him some more before swallowing him all the way. Now, she reached around to grab his buttocks while noisily slurping on his rigid shaft. Once she found a good rhythm, she licked him up and down before sucking him even harder.

Nelson grabbed her head tighter, arched his back, and exploded in her mouth. She looked up at him while licking her lips.

Someone knocked on the door.

"Get the hell away," Nelson warned loudly. "You got the wrong room."

Those words were still echoing inside the place when the door was kicked in. Clint strode forward, his gun already drawn, and said, "The funny thing is that usually I'm the one getting interrupted at moments like these."

FORTY-FIVE

"What are you doing here?" Selma asked.

Clint shook his head at her. "Shouldn't talk with your mouth full, darling."

She jumped to her feet, reached under the bed, and grabbed a knife that she'd hidden there sometime earlier. Even though she came at Clint like she meant to gut him, Selma was stopped rather easily by one of Clint's hands that he used to grab her wrist and steer her away. As she was stumbling into a wall, Nelson lunged for the pile of his clothes next to the bed.

Clint took one step forward, making certain his pistol was pointed at a spot directly between the other man's eyes. "Don't," he warned.

After thinking it over for a couple of seconds, Nelson started to grab for the pistol holstered in his gun belt which lay coiled on top of his shirt and pants. Clint put an end to Nelson's attempt to arm himself by snapping his hand forward to crack the end of his Colt's barrel against Nelson's skull. The impact made a dull crunching sound and sent Nelson to the floor in an unconscious heap.

"What are you gonna do now?" Selma asked. "Shoot an unarmed woman?"

"That's not my decision," Clint said as he stepped aside and cleared a path for another man who'd been waiting in the hallway.

"How could you do this to me?" Derrick Coates asked as he stepped into the room.

Self righteousness and rage mixed as it so often did in Selma's eyes. "You don't know that I did a damn thing to you! You're always first to accuse me, no matter what it is. I was kidnapped!"

"Is that why we found you...like this?"

"These are the same men who kidnapped those other girls," Selma explained.

"And those other times, the ransom note was sent after they were kidnapped. Not before. Honestly, Selma. Do you think I'm a fool?"

She looked away from her father to Clint. "You can't believe this. Not after we..."

"Just because I shared your bed doesn't mean I believe every word that comes out of your pretty little mouth," Clint told her. "The only reason you paid me any mind was to get me to do what you wanted. Don't you think I can tell when I'm being prodded in a certain direction?"

The insolence came right back to her face as she spat, "You didn't know anything until I was already gone!"

"You were on your way out when I found you," Clint said. "Once you were certain you'd convinced your father to pull his guards away from that shipment to guard you, you set that fire to cover your tracks so you could leave town."

"You followed me, then?"

Clint shook his head. "Didn't have to."

"I've been in the shipping business for longer than you've been alive," Coates said. "I know other men in my line of work including plenty of smugglers. All it took was a few telegrams to find out a large sale was being held right here in San Francisco. Even without those telegrams, I would've been able to tell you where anyone interested in buying or selling merchandise like that would have to be. Once we got here, Mister Adams was kind enough to do the rest."

"I've been to this beautiful city plenty of times," Clint said. "Lots of hotel owners owe me favors and none of them were very fond of the men you decided to ride with."

"These men are better than the likes of you. One's a hired killer," she said to Clint. To her father, she grunted, "And the other treats his daughter like another one of his goddamn workers. I knew when I was just a little girl that if I was to get any part of the family fortune, I'd have to take it!"

Coates shook his head, unable to say another word.

"You," Clint said, "are a spoiled little bitch who doesn't appreciate the good family she's got."

"If you grew up in my house," she told him, "you wouldn't say that."

"Sweetie," Coates said in a trembling voice. "I know we've had our differences, but—"

The shot that ripped through Coates' body came from the hallway and exploded through him in a spray of blood. His eyes remained locked on his daughter as he dropped to his knees.

FORTY-SIX

lint charged toward the doorway, not giving a damn whether or not another bullet was coming through there toward him. Judging by the surprised look on Terrance's face, he hadn't expected someone to come after him so quickly. He adjusted his aim so the pistol in his hand was pointed at Clint, but couldn't pull his trigger before Clint squeezed his.

The modified Colt bucked against Clint's palm, spitting hot lead directly into Terrance's chest. Even though he knew his first shot had been on the mark, Clint fired another to finish the job. When Terrance slammed against the closest wall, he left a wide crimson smear. Clint strode toward him down the hallway, stooping down to pluck the pistol from Terrance's hand along the way.

At the far end of the hall, another door opened and Jack Mancuso stepped outside. Without a moment's hesitation, he raised the gun in his hand and started firing. Clint managed to squeeze off a quick shot, but wasn't able to do anything more than drill a few new holes in the wall as Mancuso kept moving.

Lowering his shoulder, Mancuso charged into the room across from the one from which he'd came while shouting, "I see one hair on yer head, Adams, and I'll blow it off yer fucking shoulders!"

Clint kept his Colt at the ready and Terrance's gun in his other hand. Moving down the hall, he tested the door of the room beside the one Mancuso was using and found it to be open. Clint slipped inside and listened carefully.

"I got hostages in here!" Mancuso announced. "I'm leaving this place and if anyone gets in my way, they're dead! How much innocent blood you want on yer hands?"

Clint answered that by using Terrance's pistol to shoot straight through the wall that he and Mancuso shared. Each round made a small window into the next room. When the hammer slapped against the back of a spent round, Clint pulled his trigger one more time to make sure the sound was heard by the nearby outlaw.

Sure enough, Mancuso made his move now that he thought Clint's gun was empty. As soon as he saw the light from one of the holes in the wall become blocked by a solid shape, Clint fired a shot from his Colt through that very hole without so much as nicking the wall as it passed through.

Mancuso grunted and hit the floor with a solid thump. When Clint walked around to step into that room through the door, the outlaw was in no condition to put up much of a fight.

"Yer a maniac!" Mancuso said. "How'd you know I wasn't gonna shoot a hostage? Or how'd you know you wouldn't shoot a hostage?"

"Because," Clint replied simply. "There are no hostages to be had in this hotel."

"Right," Marshal Kaid said as he entered the room carrying handcuffs and manacles. "Because I escorted the good folks out of here while the rest of you were otherwise engaged. You might've heard something if not for all the grunting and groaning coming from your partner and the Coates girl."

"Damn whore," Mancuso snarled.

The bullet that Clint had fired through the wall that caught Mancuso hit him in the outlaw's right side. The wound wasn't in far enough to hit a lung, but was serious enough to cause a whole lot of discomfort when Kaid hit it with a swift kick. Mancuso gritted his teeth, started to curse at the Marshal, and then passed out.

"I could use an extra hand getting these men to prison," Kaid said. "Looking for work?"

Clint thought that over and nodded. "Just so long as I don't have to treat them as gentle as you do."

"Have at it," Kaid chuckled. "There is still the matter of those other robberies, kidnappings, and murders they committed. I don't know a judge in the land who'd be sympathetic if they were brought in with some bumps and bruises. Hell, if it wasn't possible that they might know of other kidnapping victims tied up somewhere, I'd kill both of these assholes right now."

"What about Selma?" Clint asked.

"What about her?"

"She can't be on the good side of the law right about now."

Looking at the wall as if he could see through it all the way to the spot where the Coates family was having their private conversation, Kaid said, "Until her father decides to say otherwise under oath, she's just another victim."

"I'll help you transporting your prisoners," Clint announced, "but only if you let me be the one to tell her what you just told me."

"When would you do that?"

"After a few days of being treated like a common criminal. I'd say she's earned that at least. She actually thought at some point she'd be able to convince me to rob her father—or kill him."

"After what she put her father through," Kaid replied, "I'm inclined to agree with you."

Clint walked back to the other room to bind Nelson's hands and feet before he woke up. When he got there, Selma was sitting on the bed and Coates was draping a blanket over her shoulders to cover her. She spat on his feet.

"Come on, Coates," Clint said, "you need a doctor."

"The bullet's in my side," he grumbled. "I'll live."

Clint took Selma by the arm and dragged her toward the door. "You've got to answer for what you've done."

Mostly, he wanted to put some distance between father and daughter. Clint hoped that some time apart might cool the fire that burned in the rift between Selma and Derrick Coates. Deep down, however, he knew it would take a lot more than that to heal the wounds that had been inflicted on that family.

San Francisco was indeed a beautiful city, but Clint was never happier to put it behind him.

ABOUT THE AUTHOR

As "J.R. Roberts" Bob Randisi is the creator and author of the long running western series, *The Gunsmith*. Under various other pseudonyms he has created and written the "Tracker," "Mountain Jack Pike," "Angel Eyes," "Ryder," "Talbot Roper," "The Son of Daniel Shaye," and "the Gamblers" Western series. His western short story collection, *The Cast-Iron Star and Other Western Stories*, is now available in print and as an ebook from Western Fictioneers Books.

In the mystery genre he is the author of the *Miles Jacoby*, *Nick Delvecchio*, *Gil & Claire Hunt*, *Dennis McQueen*, *Joe Keough*, and *The Rat Pack*, series. He has written more than 500 western novels and has worked in the Western, Mystery, Sci-Fi, Horror and Spy genres. He is the editor of over 30 anthologies. All told he is the author of over 650 novels. His arms are very, very tired.

He is the founder of the Private Eye Writers of America, the creator of the Shamus Award, the co-founder of Mystery Scene Magazine, the American Crime Writers League, Western Fictioneers and their Peacemaker Award.

In 2009 the Private Eye Writers of America awarded him the Life Achievement Award, and in 2013 the Readwest Foundation presented him with their President's Award for Life Achievement.

Made in the USA
Lexington, KY
21 December 2016